The Upside-Down Jesus
and other stories

To/ Saskia

Thanks for the support.

Kevin S.

x

First Published 2014

Copyright © Karen Jones 2014

ISBN 978-1-291-77155-8

Thanks to: The Salon and The Saloon writing groups, Get Writing, More Writing, Chapter 79, and to Catherine Baird and Rick Phoenix.

Cover design and photography by Mhairi Alexander.

Contents

The Upside-Down Jesus

Gran Reynolds moved in 'for a wee while' three months ago. She'd been not well and Mum wanted to keep an eye on her.

"We're lucky, really," Mum said. "We get to have her with us all the time."

Dad smiled. "Aye, and if we're really lucky, Gran McHendry will move in too. Then we'll have all the expert advice a family could ever wish for." Mum shoved him, playing at being annoyed. Dad laughed.

Gran Reynolds has had my bedroom the whole time – she's never been well enough to come downstairs. I'm sleeping on the couch in the front room. I pretend it's fun.

It's not fun. The couch is kid-on leather and when the sheet slides off it during the night I end up stuck to the cushions. The quilt won't stay on and I wake up cold – cold and stuck to the plastic cushions. Everyone comes into the room whenever they like; to get stuff, to watch telly, to sit for a while. It's like they forget I'm there. But I don't say anything, just in case the upside-down Jesus hears and gets even more angry with me. He's always angry.

I do like mornings in the front room. By the time I wake up, Mum has set the fire and made my breakfast, so I'm cuddly warm as I eat my toast and runny egg, all snuggled up in the quilt. I get dressed and washed in the bathroom, with the two electric bars in the heater above the door burning hot.

I'm still at the wee school, so I just have to walk up the road. My brothers are at the big school and have to get the bus. I don't want to go to the big school. Buses make me sick. They smell bad and the drivers are rubbish; they brake suddenly, for no reason – or maybe when they see a lassie they fancy. They seem to fancy a lot of lassies. Whatever school I'm at, I'll still have to pass the upside-down Jesus.

Dad gives me a big squeezy hug before he leaves, the brothers ruffle my hair or push me over – depends what kind of mood they're in. Mum always has to strip Gran's bed 'cause she's messed it during the night. You can smell it right through the house.

I have to go in and see Gran before I go. I take a big deep breath in the front room, run out the door and up the stairs into my old room, kiss Gran's cheek, let the breath out, shout, "Bye!" and hold my breath until I'm downstairs again. I grab my bag and dive out the front door into the fresh air, Mum yelling after me, "Did you say goodbye to Gran?" Gran shouts, "Aye she did – she always does. Kirsty's a good wean."

I skip up the road. It's not that I like school; it's just good to be out of the house, away from Mum's sad eyes and Gran's bad smell. She was brilliant before she was ill, my gran. She used to teach us to bake, take us on days out, buy us sweets. Not like Gran McHendry. Gran McHendry is scary, and she likes being scary. She likes to take her teeth out and show us her mangled gums. She doesn't like us to make any noise – sometimes she says we breathe too loud. She makes grey mince full of hard carrots and stringy onions. We have to eat it or we get a skelp. She eats Parma Violets. She's the only person in the world who doesn't think Parma Violets are horrible, so she must be evil.

Halfway up the road I slow down. Halfway up the road is the path down to the old abandoned garage. Half way up the road is where the angry upside-down Jesus is. He's in that garage. I know he is. I've never seen him, but one day, if I'm really bad, those doors will swing open and he'll be there, stuck to that cross, upside down, eyes staring, teeth bared, angry at me for not being good after all he's suffered for me.

I cross the road so I'm opposite the path. I don't look at the path, don't look at the garage. I never look. Well, I try not to, but I can't stop my eyes from wandering, from wanting to see the upside-down Jesus. When I feel my eyes move that way, I run. I run like I'm being chased. I run to the end of the road, breathless, sweating, even though it's not that far.

While I stand and wait to cross the road, I see Mrs Adams working in the shop opposite. She smiles and waves. That's when I know I'm safe. If the angry Jesus was behind me on the upside-down cross, she wouldn't smile and wave – she'd look scared or shocked or at least a wee bit surprised, wouldn't she? I look behind me, just in case she's in cahoots with the Jesus. I do it every morning. He's never there; she's always smiling and waving. But I have to check, 'cause you never know.

On the way to school I meet the "worthies" – that's what Dad calls them – the women who go to mass every morning, even though they don't have to. I think that's mad, my brothers think it's "desperate". Mum kid-on skelps us if we say it's mad or desperate. Dad says those women have been seventy-five years old since he was a boy. Mum says that's proof going to mass every morning gets you a long life. Dad says what's the point in having a long life if all you do is spend your bloody time at mass. Mum kid-on skelps him for swearing in front of us. We giggle. Dad's funny – Mum's funny too, but in a different way.

The worthies all dress the same – checked coats, hats with weird wee stalks coming out the top, rain-mates if it's wet, brown tights and flat shoes. The smelly powder they put on their faces gets stuck in all the wrinkles and their false teeth are yellow. Gran McHendry is a worthy. Gran Reynolds isn't that keen on the chapel or the new priest – she says he's the worst kind, from the backside of the backend of the backwoods. They ask how Gran Reynolds is doing. They already know, 'cause Gran McHendry tells them, but they ask me so I'll go home and tell Mum and Gran Reynolds that they asked. Dad says all their good deeds have to be noticed and appreciated.

When I tell them she's fine, they hold their heads to one side, smile and give each other strange looks. They walk off, muttering about "shame … sick … not long now". I want to shout that she's not that bloody ill, but that would make the upside-down Jesus really mad at me, so I ignore them and go to school, hoping I don't get Mr Taggart for RE.

Mr Taggart is the one who told us about the upside-down Jesus in the first place. Well, it wasn't really about a Jesus – it was about a saint who had been crucified upside down, which was, apparently, worse than being crucified the right way up – I couldn't see why, but I didn't ask. But in my head, it was a Jesus, 'cause there are all the Jesus pictures everywhere, and I can see his faces dead clear, so the upside-down crucified man always has a Jesus face.

Mr Taggart hates me and always finds a reason to make me stand out at the front of class, facing the blackboard. I don't really mind facing the blackboard. It's easier to block out what he's saying if you can't see his face. It's always scary stuff about torment, the bad fire and eternal suffering. Gran Reynolds says him and the new priest must have been born in the same street.

It is him this morning – I see his cord jacket hanging just inside the classroom door. It's going to be another bad day.

Today's lesson is about some poor saint who was beaten and burned and other terrible things. But at least no one hung her upside down. At least she's not angry with me for not being good after all she's suffered

That was the first time Mr Taggart made me face the board – the day I said I never asked anyone to suffer for me. I didn't mean to be cheeky, I just meant that I would never want anyone to be in pain for me – never ever – and especially not in all the terrible ways the Christians used to find to torture each other. Mr Taggart says they were righteous, but a bit overenthusiastic. Gran Reynolds says that's like saying Hitler was a bit intolerant. I wasn't sure what that meant, but Dad laughed himself off his chair.

I think about all the funny things Dad and Gran Reynolds say, and that helps me get through RE without having to face the board. I get picked for ten mental and get every one right. I get through reading without a mistake and without a stammer. I get through gym without falling off any of the apparatus. I get through lunch without being force-fed custard. I get through sewing without stitching my fingers to anything – that's very unusual. I sing my heart out in music and carry the last note in 'Our Lady of Aberdeen' longer than anyone else in the class. Miss Lennox takes me aside and reminds me that I play triangle for a reason, and could I maybe sing a wee bit quieter in future. I smile. She squeezes my arm and says there's nothing to beat enthusiasm. It's a good day.

I skip my way home again, until I reach the path to the garage. It's been such a good day, I decide I'm not going to run. I'm going to 'face my fear'. I'll walk slowly past the upside-down Jesus' garage and he can glare at me all he wants. I stand straight and tall, the way they teach us in gym, I take a deep breath and I walk slow and steady. I turn and look at the garage – it's just a garage, there's nothing in there but old scrap and some cobwebs. I can feel my heart thumping in my chest and I want to scream, but I don't. I take a few steps down the path – I don't need to do this, I never need to go down this path, but I do it anyway. I stand, I stare, I dare the upside-down Jesus to spring those doors open and let a roar out at me. Nothing happens.

I walk away, trying to stay calm. Then I run. I run faster than I ever thought I could. I run up the garden path, into the house, into the kitchen, yelling, "Mum, Mum – I'm home!" Dad is in the kitchen. He should be at work. He holds his arms out to me. I walk into them, accept the hug, though I don't know why I deserve it – he doesn't know about my good day or the upside-down Jesus not roaring at me.

"Mum's not in, pet. She's at the hospital with Gran Reynolds. You and the boys are going to Gran McHendry's for tea."

"Is she making mince?" I screw up my face.

Dad smiles. "Aye, probably – so long as she doesn't try her hand at dough balls, you'll all survive. You might be staying there overnight, okay?"

We've never stayed at Gran McHendry's. "Why? I don't want to – I don't like it there. It smells of Parma Violets." It's true – it's like walking into the worst sweetie shop in the world.

"I know. But it's just for one night. And when you get back, you'll have your old room again."

I think for a minute. "But where will Gran Reynolds sleep when she's back from hospital? Are they making her better? Is she going back to her own house?"

"No, pet, she won't be able …" I've never seen him cry before. It looks like his face has had an earthquake – all those creases appear from nowhere and surprise us both.

I hug him closer. "It's okay, Daddy – I don't mind sleeping in the front room. Gran Reynolds can come back here when she's out of hospital."

He hugs me so tight I can't breathe. When he stops crying he lets me go. "You're a good wean, aren't you, Kirsty?"

I smile. "That's what Gran Reynolds says, and she's always right. She says that too." Dad half laughs, half cries, so it comes out like a bark. We both laugh then.

I am a good wean, and the upside-down Jesus can think what he likes. I never asked him to suffer for me, so why should I suffer for him? It's a good day, one I'm sure I'll never forget.

Pictures of Lily

In the first shot, Lily is dancing, head thrown back, eyes closed, hair falling away from her face, her lips parted in a smile that's about to break into a laugh. I'm almost in the picture, just behind the guy who's reaching for her hand but, most importantly, I'm not the guy who's reaching for her hand. I'm not the guy who's supposed to be in the picture. I'm strictly background.

It was just luck that I was in the uni canteen the day her phone slipped out of her pocket and skittered under her chair. The place is always so noisy – pot lids clattering, trays falling, people talking – she didn't notice, didn't hear it land. No one did. Once she walked away I moved quickly, scooped it up, started after her, glad of this opportunity to actually talk to her. Then I stopped.

The next frame is one of those Facebook selfie profile pictures. When I see those, I always assume the user has no friends, is so pathetic they had to be their own photographer, their arms stretched, distancing themselves from their loneliness, a false smile etched on a sad face. I took my profile pic with my iPhone, so I know what I'm talking about. But Lily has lots of these shots. She experiments with poses, outfits, looking up from under her fringe, or wide-eyed and fake-honest into the lens.

In my favourite picture, she's lying on her side on her bed. She's wearing a vest top and shorts. There's a teddy bear on her pillow, its feet just visible above her head. Her hair splays out around her and the act of raising her arm at this angle to take the picture has pushed her breasts up and together, making them look fuller and rounder than they really are – than they probably are – and her gaze is steady, as though daring the viewer to look away. I wonder if she thought about the juxtaposition of the cuddly toy and her pose, the contrast between innocence and sexuality. Something

11

tells me she did. Something tells me nothing Lily does is by chance. I look at that picture more often than I should. I feel guilty afterwards.

I've copied all of her photographs, memos and contacts. I will give the phone back, but not just yet. She's had it blocked since she lost it and I've taken out the sim in case it could be traced, so all I'm hanging on to is a useless piece of pink plastic. But it lived in her pocket. She used it, touched it for so long, it makes me feel close to her.

I should speak to her. I really think I should speak to her. I should have given the phone back straight away, that was my best chance. If I do it now it'll look weird. I've had it for a week. I could tell her I found it, heard she'd lost hers. Or I could say nothing.

Her Facebook account is set to private, but I managed to get in before she blocked the phone, so now I'll be able to see all her check-ins. I'll engineer a meeting with Lily soon. I just have to work out how to get her alone, how to get her to look at me, to laugh with me, the way she does with the guy who was reaching for her hand, the guy who isn't me.

And when I finally talk to her I'll have to remember to forget everything I've learned. Forget her dog's name, that she likes snowboarding, how her brothers tower over her and look more like her parents than she does. I'll have to forget that while people like me, people she's never noticed, think her name is Kate, the people she loves call her by her middle name. I'll have to forget her name is Lily.

The Resurrection of Andy McPhail

Andy McPhail opened his eyes, struggling against lids that felt glued shut. A chemical smell shot up his nose, almost strong enough to depilate nasal hairs, and stung when it hit the back of his throat, making him gag. Thomas Hendry hovered over him, a confused look on his big, slack-jawed face – though to be fair, Thomas always looked confused.

Thomas raised his eyebrows and snorted a tiny laugh. "Well, this is a turn up for the books, eh?"

Andy sat up, ignoring the white sheet that slipped down and revealed his nakedness, more concerned with the rest of his surroundings: lying on a metal table; Thomas Hendry wearing a rubber apron and long rubber gloves; chemical smells; plastic tubing – lots of plastic tubing. He looked back down at the white sheet. Time to call a shroud a shroud.

He pulled the sheet up to his chin. "What the fuck's going on?"

"Eh, you're dead, mate. Or at least you were. Totally. Definitely. I was just about to start the procedures." He waved his gloved hands in front of Andy's face, then hid something that looked like a wine bottle stopper behind his back. "Just as well you woke up when you did or it would have been really sore."

Andy ran his fingers through his hair and slapped some feeling back into his face. "What happened? When did it happen?"

Thomas puffed out his cheeks and rolled his eyes to the ceiling. "Sudden death, night before last, fatal heart attack."

"Heart attack? I'm only thirty-four. I'm too young for a heart attack. And by the way, it clearly wasn't fatal."

Thomas shrugged. "S'what the doc said, so here you are."

"Aye, here I am, very much alive. What do we do now?"

"I dunno – this has never happened before, or at least not since I started working for my dad. I suppose you should go home. Sarah'll be pleased to see you."

"Do you not think you should call somebody? The police maybe?"

"No law against being alive, mate. Naw, you get away home. I'll explain to my dad what happened. He'll be a bit pissed off, mind. We could really have done with the money. Things have been a bit slow recently."

Andy's brow furrowed. "Oh. Well, I'll apologise next time I see him." He waited for Thomas to offer some practical help. He gave up. "Have you got any of my clothes?"

Thomas looked around. "Sure. Sarah left a bag with stuff she wanted you buried in. It's here somewhere." He found the bag and handed it to Andy. Navy blue suit, white shirt, black shoes and a pencil-thin black tie. She always tried to make him look like one of those daft boys in The Beatles. He'd refused the haircut. He'd specifically asked to be buried in his work clothes, given he was sure the coal face would eventually kill him, but what he'd wanted clearly didn't matter any more in death than it did in life.

"Eh, a wee bit of privacy while I get dressed, mate?"

"What? Oh, aye, sure. Though you've no secrets from me now – a cavity search is first order of business." Thomas smiled and turned his back.

Christ, as if being declared dead wasn't bad enough, Thomas Hendry had had his fingers up his jacksy. Actually, death seemed preferable. He wondered if the cavity search really was first order of business or just a predilection of Thomas's, then his mind drifted back to the thing that looked like a wine bottle stopper. He shuddered and dressed as quickly as he could.

"Right, that's me ready. I'll away then." He felt in his pockets – nothing, not even a ha'penny. Of course not. It's not like Sarah expected him to pay a ferryman. Too far to walk home, though, especially feeling weak and in this stupid suit and pointy shoes. "Sorry to be a pain, Thomas, but is there any chance of a lift home?"

Thomas jumped to attention. "Of course. What am I thinking? Aye, sure you had the cars booked anyway. Using one a couple of days early, but what the hell, eh?"

In the car, Andy tried to persuade Thomas to get past twenty on the speedometer, but he didn't seem capable of driving faster. The lingering smell of wood and flowers reminded Andy of how close he'd come to travelling in the back. When they reached the main street he grabbed Thomas's arm.

"Listen, I think I'll just walk from here. Take in some fresh air, remind myself how lucky I am to be alive."

The hearse shuddered to a halt.

"Okay. Oh, Sarah'll be that pleased to see you. She was awful upset. We thought the doc would have to give her something to calm her down. Screaming, sobbing – hysterical, so she was."

"Really?"

"Oh, aye. Devastated. Totally devastated."

Andy looked sceptical. He got out of the car and waved Thomas off into the morning light. He looked along the quiet street. The village looked smaller, dirtier; the cottages less quaint. He saw Samuel, the local baker, getting out of his van. There was something familiar about the red plaid shirt he was wearing.

Samuel looked at him closely. "Andy? I thought you were dead?"

"Aye, that's what everyone thinks. I'll be having a serious word with Doctor Ainsley."

"So you're not dead?"

"Eh, no, it was a mistake. I'm fine."

Samuel nodded, satisfied. "Good for you, son. Right, I better get back to work." He opened the door to the shop and the smell of freshly baked bread washed over Andy. He hoped Sarah would have some food in. Of course she would – she'd have been feeding the visitors who'd come to pay their respects. But the smell of that bread was so good.

He called after Samuel, "Any chance of a loaf? I've no money right now – just got off the slab in Hendry's, wasn't really expecting this, know what I mean?"

Samuel smiled. "Sure, son. Least I can do." He came back with a freshly baked bloomer.

Andy looked more closely at the plaid shirt, the torn left pocket, just like his shirt. No, she couldn't have – not that quickly.

Samuel patted him on the shoulder and handed him the loaf. "There you go."

The smell and the heat from the bread filled Andy with happiness. He forgot about the shirt. This tiny thing, this bread, suddenly meant everything. "You're a gentleman, sir."

"No bother. Sure, you can drop the money off later."

Andy smiled. Even being a walking miracle wouldn't get you a free meal from Sam.

He tore off chunks of bread and let out a moan of pleasure as he chewed. It was perfect – the only thing he'd ever want to eat again, he was sure.

He'd slowed his pace. He should have been hurrying home, hurrying back to Sarah, but he couldn't be sure how she'd take his reappearance. In the past few years their married life had gone as stale as Samuel's 'special offers'. They wanted different things, to be in different places, to live different lives. They rarely spoke, their sex life had turned into a seaside postcard joke – only on Saturday nights and over as quickly as possible. She faked it, dutifully – he had started to do the same. If she noticed – and surely she must have noticed – she didn't comment. In the last few weeks they hadn't even bothered going through the motions. It wasn't worth the two minutes of effort. Their tenth anniversary just a few weeks away, he'd wondered if they'd make it. He almost hadn't.

But Thomas said she'd been upset – no, devastated – at the news of his death. Maybe this, his resurrection, would be the catalyst for a new start. Maybe he'd finally get her to move away from this dump. She loved everything about cities – the fashion, the restaurants, the busy streets – but was too set in her ways to leave where they'd both been born and raised. Too afraid to actually live where there was life. Maybe now he'd be able to convince her that they should grab this second chance. He straightened his shoulders, smoothed down his suit jacket and quickened his step.

"Andy?" Judith Kelsey, self-professed clairvoyant, looked surprised to see him.

"Yep, it's me."

"Well you're back early. I wasn't expecting you for a couple of weeks, you know, after you'd settled in."

"Eh, I'm not actually dead, Mrs Kelsey. It was a mistake. I'm fine. I'm on my way home now."

Mrs Kelsey cocked her head to one side and sighed. "Aw, son, I'm sorry you've not accepted it yet. It happens sometimes. Though I'm not sure how you managed to get back so fast. That'll be the problem." She addressed her next comments to the air, slightly to the left and over his head. "What were you thinking of, letting him through so soon? It's not like he died a violent death – it was just his heart gave out. I'll be having a word with your superiors."

He reached out and patted her arm. "Mrs Kelsey, it really was a mistake. See? You can feel me touching you. I'm real."

Mrs Kelsey tutted. "Well of course I can feel you touch me – I'm gifted, daft boy. Now, Sarah'll not be able to see you, so don't be getting upset and thinking she's ignoring you. You should go back now – wait a while."

Andy laughed and shook his head. "I'll see you soon, Mrs Kelsey."

"Not too soon, son, not too soon."

He tore another chunk off the loaf. "Actually, Mrs Kelsey, could I trouble you for some water?"

She looked at the bread in his hands. "How are you managing to do that? You're an awful fast learner, and you were never that bright when you were alive. No offence intended."

"Some taken, but a wee drink would help wash this down nicely."

She went into her house, glancing at him over her shoulder, as if he might disappear at any second, and returned with a plastic cup full of water.

"Cheers. I'll get the cup back to you tomorrow." Andy sipped at the drink. The coolest, clearest, cleanest thing in the world. He even liked the cup, the floral pattern – perfect for picnics. Just like the ones he'd bought for Sarah before she'd declared she hated picnics. Just a few more minutes and he'd be at his front door. Would she throw herself into his arms? Hug him, kiss him, hold him like she'd never let him leave her side again? The other things he'd taken for granted now seemed so important, seeing Sarah would be best of all.

"Andy?"

Hannah Tierney. His first love. His oldest friend and now Sarah's best friend. One of the many things sacrificed to his marriage.

"But I thought …"

"Aye, you and everyone else – one of you might have tried to give me the kiss of life."

"We did. I did. I don't get it. What's going on?"

Andy shrugged. "No idea. I woke up in Hendry's. Thomas wasn't best pleased to see me – not good for the profit margins. So you were there? I don't remember anything. What happened?"

Hannah leaned back against the wall of her house to steady herself. Andy was relieved to finally see someone shaken by his reappearance.

"We were at the miners' welfare – the fund raising night for the school gym – they were about to call the raffle when you collapsed. We tried to get you back. Doc Ainsley was in the public bar, so he came through and checked you out. He said there was nothing we could do. You were gone. There was talk of getting an ambulance, getting the city involved, but everyone agreed you'd want things kept local, so Doc signed the certificate and …" She bit her lip, a habit he used to love, but now found irritating.

"And?"

"Well, we put you in the wee hall. The raffle still had to be called, and Tam Hendry was drunk, so he couldn't drive you back to the parlour, and Thomas isn't allowed to drive at night, so …"

"So you carried on with the do? Seriously?"

She shrugged. "Ach, you know what it's like around here – nothing stops a party."

"And Sarah?"

"We phoned her. She came down, got everything organized for the next day with the Hendrys. She seemed fine at first, then she lost her cool right in the middle of the hall. It was weird. I mean she really, completely lost it."

Andy's eyes narrowed. "You were surprised?"

"Well, you know, she's not one for public displays of emotion, eh?"

"But the love of her life had just died, Hannah"

Hannah looked at her boots, scuffing the left toe on the pavement. He wanted to ask more but wasn't sure he'd like the answers. He turned and walked away, his belief in the brand new start faltering. It was still worth a try though – 'til death do us part and all that – and he really, really wasn't dead.

Hannah called after him. "Andy! Hang on!" She went in to the house, came back and handed him a bottle of wine.

"What's this for?"

"You won the raffle."

He took the bottle and then burst out laughing. "This is some fuckin' place."

"Aye, you were better off out of it, pal." She ruffled his hair, pecked him on the cheek and went back inside. Her perfume lingered. The perfume he'd bought Sarah for her birthday. He knew Hannah would phone Sarah.

Yards from their front door his chest felt tight. He hoped it wasn't his heart again. If it had ever been his heart – he wouldn't trust Doc Ainsley with a pet goldfish. He fought to breathe, struggled to walk. He drew level with the house. A curtain twitched. One eye watched him. She knew. She knew but she didn't run to the door, out into the street, into his arms. He stared at the window, willed her to care, to give them a chance at a new life. Nothing.

He straightened up and walked on past. The pains eased off and he smiled. He broke the neck of the wine bottle against a wall. He raised the bottle and toasted the rest of his death – may it be better than the life he'd never really lived. Andy McPhail closed his eyes, tipped his head back, felt the delicious wine drip down his throat and never looked back.

The Truth About Snow

Dear Kaoru,

When I found the box in a moth-eaten bag in the attic, I remembered you. I doubt you'll remember me – it's been almost forty years, after all. You were my first pen-friend, provided (forced on me, truth be told) by my first year English teacher.

I envied my friends who got girls from Sweden, Spain, Holland – places I felt I could relate to. But Japan? I didn't know what to do with you, how to talk to you. You were just too alien to me. Did Scotland – did I – seem the same to you?

With hindsight you were amazing. Had I been remotely interested, I'd have learned so much about a country of which I knew nothing. You sent me beautiful gifts: the box with the embroidered lid; a tiny carved animal (I don't remember what kind); picture postcards of your village; photos of you dressed in traditional garb, like a tiny Geisha, with beautiful shining hair and a spectacularly white smile.

I sent you dull accounts of my days, tried to interest you in Donny Osmond and David Cassidy and platform shoes. Sent you a picture of me in Bay City Rollers trousers and jumper (all in purple, because that was Donny Osmond's favourite colour – I wasn't faithful to anyone at that age). But all you really wanted was what you had given – a taste of a different country, different culture. In particular, you were obsessed with snow. You'd never seen it in your part of the country, never smelt it, never touched it. You just wanted to know about snow.

I could have told you about streets stunned to silence under its white sheet. I could have told you about snowball fights, hands so cold they're hot, faces sore from windburn and laughter. I could have told you about feeling like an astronaut every time you were the first to make a footprint in a fresh fall.

I told you it was cold, it turned to wet, dirty slush, and then I stopped writing, ignored your letters.

So I got my wish, got my Swedish girl and all she talked about was boys and sex – real boys, real sex, not just pop stars on glossy posters – way beyond my ken. Then I got a bossy German girl who got annoyed if my letters didn't arrive promptly. I'd tell you about the Russian girl, but then I'd have to kill you. My pen-friends were like a united nations of crass stereotypes. I gave up.

I should have stuck with you, Kaoru. You asked for so little and I gave you less. I just wish I had told you the truth about snow.
With regards and regrets,
Karen

Diamond Dust and Moonstones

His chest hair, more red than blond – how could I have forgotten that? – irritates and tickles my nose with every inhalation as he holds me tightly, my head pressed against him. He smells sour and over-ripe – evidence of his long journey and insistence that he couldn't hold off, couldn't take the few minutes to shower. I want to pull away, to get as far away from here, from this, from him as I can. He strokes my hair; his hands are squarer, heavier than I remember. In my mind he was always the artist, the musician. His palms soft, fingers long and elegant. These hands that touch me now and make me shudder rather than shiver with pleasure, are hands more suited to a bricklayer.

He is still an artist and musician but his money comes from his day job, from real estate. And he has plenty of money, more than this grim hotel room would suggest. It was the first place we came to on our walk away from our pilgrimage to The Palomino Club, the scene of our first kiss twenty-five years ago. The club is still there, music drifting out into the street, but the sign has lost most of its letters and the few that are left hang precariously, faded and neglected; the ubiquitous wear and tear of the old, not worth repairing. We didn't go in – we just looked at the fat, crooked letters reflected in the dirty puddle outside the door and shook our heads at how sad they looked. He didn't want to walk any further than this place after that; the only thing from our past he said he really wanted was me, naked.

"I still can't quite believe this. Can you? Can you believe this?" He's slightly out of breath from his exertions. "Rhona?"

His voice doesn't carry the cultured tones I remember. Far superior to my broad dialect, he had a voice that captivated me, promised things and places I had only imagined. When I tracked him down through old college friends and contacted him, it was by letter, so I had no way of knowing that the voice I'd heard in my frequent fantasies has gone, like the rest of him, downhill, skewed by the accent of his chosen home in America, but not far enough to be one thing or the other. More mongrel than hybrid, it grates.

My own voice is clipped, unnatural to my ears. "No. No, it's quite unbelievable."

"I never thought I'd get the chance to be with you again. I've thought about it – I've thought about it a lot – the sex was always spectacular. It was everything else that was screwed up, eh?"

He laughs. A pleased with himself laugh.

I feel like I might vomit. I think about a few moments ago, to the rough, frantic coupling, when I winced and struggled not to shout my disgust as a drop of sweat fell from the end of his nose and splashed onto my forehead. It's not just physical repulsion – and I do find him repulsive – there's something else. Guilt? No, I feel no guilt. I no longer have anyone to feel guilty about. But shame. I do feel shame. I've allowed myself to only remember the good parts of us. Tonight, here with him in this hovel, the minute he touched me the bad bullied its way back to the surface. I should have stopped him.

"Yes, well, you were never one for fidelity. That can be problematic in a relationship." It slips out. I wish I could claw it back. It doesn't matter now. It's not like I'm planning to see him again, not as if we're about to try again, but I don't want him to see it still hurts. Until a moment ago, I didn't know it did.

My hair feels the full blast of his snort of derision and a fresh wave of revulsion washes over me.

"Not exactly one to talk, are you? Unless you're going to tell me Brendan knows you're here tonight, fucking me for old time's sake."

The pain at hearing him use Brendan's name winds me. "No. No he has no idea."

"There you go then. And at least you and I were never married."

Silence. Silence except for the dripping tap in the miniscule, mouldy wet-room. I went in there earlier, thinking if I freshened up, he'd do the same. The water had left a brown stain in the green sink. Avocado, that's the colour. My parents had that suite in the 70s. Everyone did, even his parents. No one has it anymore. It's all white now. I'm convinced we've managed to find the only hotel in Glasgow with a tasteless reminder of our childhood. We've also found old scabs to pick at and it's happened a lot faster than I thought it would.

"So how is old Brendan? Still working?"

"He wasn't that much older than me."

He grabs the loose, stretch-marked skin around my belly. "Well you're showing signs of having been around for a while, doll, so fair question."

His attempt at slipping into an accent he never had is more offensive than his words. It always was. Raised by English parents, sent to private school in Glasgow, he remained virtually accentless.

So many repressed recollections battle for my attention. How he balked at the street I lived in when he first visited: "A council house? Really?" He had never been in one, couldn't get over how tiny it was, couldn't help letting my family see his amusement.

But I also recall how happy he was when he took me to the café where I had my first croissant, my first cappuccino. He took me to see bands I'd never heard of, subtitled films, plays I'd never have thought to see. So many firsts with my first. Those are the memories that have sustained me over the years. But he tired of it, of me, and his pleasure at showing me new things grew to scorn of my ignorance and innocence. How have I managed to forget the reality of what we were in the end?

"I had children. My body changed. It happens. I'm happy with it as it is now."

He grabs at the loose skin again. "With this? You're happy with this? Oh, let me guess, you're still pretending to be a feminist and this shows you've lived, you've loved, you're a real woman?" He laughs again.

I swing my legs off the bed, glad he didn't give me the chance to remove my stockings earlier – I don't want to put bare feet on this carpet. He reaches for my shoulder.

"Aw, come on. I'm only joking. We've turned out pretty well, you and me. You look fantastic for your age. We both do. Let's not fight. I get the feeling you're only going to give me tonight, so let's not waste it."

Fantastic for our age. His face is heavily lined and too tanned. He clearly enjoys his food more than is healthy or wise and his nose is red from too much booze. His eyes are dull, his hair thinning and those hands. What happened to his hands?

"I'm not fighting, I just have to leave."

I hear him slump back down onto his pillow.

"Oh, I remember this now. I remember your sllences, your huffs that could last for days. And you wonder why I looked elsewhere for fun?"

I turn to look at him one last time. "But you stayed with me. You came back to me each time."

He shrugs. "Like I said, the sex was great. Still is, eh?" He reaches out to me. "We can at least have a bit more fun since I came all this way. What do you say?"

I say goodbye, not just to him, to the romantic notion that one day he, my true love, would come back and take me with him. Now all I can think is, Brendan might have been boring – or was he just safe, nice? – but he genuinely loved me, adored me. Jesus – a romanticised version of Brendan is already taking shape in my mind. I shake my head – waiting for someone who can't come back would be too ridiculous, even by my standards.

Outside, I push my scarf up around my chin, more aware of jowls and wattle and gravity's pull after an evening with someone who always saw my faults. I huddle into my coat – the one my daughter calls my funeral coat – and walk back to my empty house.

The night is cold and the pavement, if you're in the right mood, looks like it's speckled with diamond dust and moonstones. Tonight all I see is silver frost and trampled, discarded chewing gum.

Limits of Love

Clothes, duvet, photographs – his beautiful eyes, staring – she watched the flames grow higher, but held onto his lies:

Dear Mum

Thanks for the cigarettes – the shaving foam, too. Don't think I'll use it. Don't want to look too pretty. Why didn't you just bring them on your next visit?

Look, we didn't get a chance to talk after the sentencing. I need to explain

You used to say that, with my eyes, I'd have all the girls running after me, remember? Well that's what happened. I know she was only eleven, but she knew what she was doing – just like the last one. They all know.

I know you believe me – it's what keeps me sane.

Thanks, Mum.

See you soon.

Davy.

She threw the letter on the fire and rubbed her smoke-filled eyes, wiping at tears, memories, and guilt that would never go away.

Buried

She peeled the potatoes and let the skins fall to the floor and mingle with the remnants of previous meals.

The laundry mountain teetered on the table top, poised to join the trash on the mud-smeared linoleum.

His snores echoed through the tiny house, his breath pungent enough to tinge the foetid air with an acrid taste she could never quite shift.

But nothing masked the stench of failure that seeped up through the floorboards, taunting her: the stress she'd been unable to endure; the chances she'd never taken, even if he'd let her.

All those children who had never been, yet always would be, under her feet.

Necromancy

I lay her out the way I did the others, and before rigor mortis sets in; naked, on her back, right leg bent so that the inside of the right foot rests against the left thigh. Her right arm is across her flat belly, left hand resting on the left thigh.

This one is so fresh, so fragrant – only minutes since her grateful last sigh. I lie down beside her in that same position – the position I've slept in since childhood. We look like we were meant to be together.

In a few hours the spell will work and she'll speak to me. She would never have spoken to me when she was alive, but when I wake her she will howl my name and shriek and curse, filling me with passion.

Sometimes the others come back – seven girls berating me. Those are the best nights, when the pleasure is almost too great. And when they and I are spent, I lie down by my latest love and the others fade away.

The sound of innocent girlish laughter floating through my window from the college campus lulls me to sleep, and dreams of the next time.

Past Perfect

Billy Fairlie cradled the perfectly formed dog turd in his hand as though it was a precious item to be cherished and protected. When he reached Lisa Denton's door he hid his surprise behind his back and rang the bell. The varnished door opened.

Mrs Denton shuddered when she saw Billy's mud-smeared face and stringy hair, then turned and yelled her daughter's name.

Lisa leapt down the stairs, her blonde hair bouncing around her shoulders. She came to an abrupt halt when she saw him, eyebrows raised quizzically over blue, glistening eyes. Billy smiled.

Mrs Denton could wait no more. "What do you want?" She hissed the words, afraid the neighbours would hear a Fairlie at her door.

Billy grinned, produced the dog turd and split it in two. He handed half to Lisa, then bit into his portion. Lisa smiled and followed suit. Mrs Denton screamed. Billy grabbed Lisa's hand and they ran, howls of laughter escaping their brown-smeared mouths.

They were six years old. The dog turd was a chocolate fake. She had passed the test and he would love her forever.

#

Approaching Glasgow airport, Billy smiled as the thirty-year-old prank came to mind. Twenty years had passed since he'd last seen Lisa – the girl for whom he would never be good enough. The teenager whose every word, every move could make Billy catch his breath: as if not breathing would freeze her in that moment. Twenty years since he'd run away from the pain of losing her.

Until he received the letter he'd believed that his parents had been right to send him to live with his aunt in Toronto. He hadn't argued with their decision – he'd welcomed it. If he couldn't be with Lisa, then what did it matter where he lived? His life in

Canada, his marriage to Ellen, his business – the letter had made it all melt away. He'd packed a bag with old clothes his wife wouldn't miss, added a couple of good suits he kept at the office and travelled first class, Toronto to Glasgow.

Why now, he wondered? After all these years, why had she written? There was little detail in the letter; she hadn't even given her address, just a phone number. What stood out, what made him buy a ticket and head for home, was the line, "I've thought about you constantly Billy, all these years."

As Billy re-read Lisa's letter, the descent began.

#

Her family had moved when she was sixteen; moved to get away from him. 'Scum from the scheme', her mother had called him. How he wished he'd been smart enough to call her 'trash with cash'. The Dentons came from nothing – rumour had it they'd won the pools – but she treated him and everyone else from the council estate like dirt under her feet. She couldn't separate them, so she took Lisa away. It was only to Perth, but it might as well have been the moon for someone in Billy's position. No money, no family car, no address to look up. Her mother had been careful to leave no trace. But Lisa could have contacted him; he had stayed in the same house for months after she left. Why hadn't she tried?

He got a taxi from the airport to his parents' house. They had remained in the village, bought their council house, retired into a comfortable existence. The house looked different – smaller, somehow – but his key still took him back to his childhood.

"Billy! Ellen's been on the phone, she's worried sick. What's going on? Ach, come here and give me a hug."

Billy smiled. His mother would, thank God, never change. He grabbed her and cuddled her, breathing in the talc, the Ellnet hairspray, and the sausages she'd cooked for tea.

He laughed. "I just had a sudden hankering for some square sausage, Mum."

She couldn't help laughing with him, but then shoved him away. "Seriously, what's up?"

His father called from the living room. "Is that our Billy? Come in here."

Billy smiled, did as he was told. His father dropped his newspaper on the table, looked Billy up and down and shook his head.

"Well, look at you." He grabbed Billy and almost squeezed the life out of him. "It's good to see you, son – been a while, eh?' He released Billy from the hug, but held on to his shoulders and nodded. "So, you've come looking for Lisa?"

Billy didn't know who looked more surprised at the question, him or his mother.

"Lisa? Lisa Denton? Why would he be looking for her? Is there something I don't know? Something Ellen doesn't know?"

Billy felt a pang of guilt. His mother thought Ellen was perfect, so how could he tell her their relationship had been hanging together by a frayed thread for the past couple of years? Arguments over starting a family, over the hours he worked, over the time he spent in the pub, followed by silences that could last for weeks. He'd tried to love her – he *had* loved her, as best he could – just not the way he'd always loved Lisa.

"Dad, how did you know I was here for Lisa?"

His mother wasn't giving up. "What's the point to all this? We don't even know where she is now. She stopped sending the letters …"

"Agnes, the boy has to do this. Every phone call, he's asked about her."

Billy stared at them. "Letters?"

"Way back, son, she used to send letters here, wanted us to forward them to you. Your mother and I couldn't see what good it would do."

"So you just didn't bother to tell me she was looking for me? Unbelievable."

His father raised his hands in surrender. "We were wrong, son, but I'm trying to help you now. I saw her last week, gave her your address – I take it that's why you're here? She wrote to you?"

"Yeah, she did. Am I supposed to thank you?"

"Well, we'll see how you feel about that later. Are you going to see her?"

"I haven't got her address – I'll have to call her first. I'd rather just turn up and surprise her."

"No, she wouldn't have given you the address, but I have it."

His mother looked fit to burst. "You've got her address? Why would you ...?"

"Agnes, you can shout at me when Billy's gone. Let's just get this over with, let him get it out of his system." He handed Billy the address. "She's not the lassie you knew, just don't expect too much." He settled down into his favourite chair. "We'll be here for you when you get home."

#

Billy took a taxi to her address, not surprised she hadn't written it in the letter – if the area was anything like it had been in his youth, he'd need an armed escort. His father's words annoyed him: get it out of his system, get it over with. Like Lisa was some sort of disease, some sort of poison or chore.

The taxi pulled up in front of a grey tenement. Some of the windows were boarded up, some had steel shutters. Kids played in the streets; filthy kids whose clothes were too light for the late September chill; kids who should have been in bed hours ago. He paid the fare and the cab shot off into the distance.

He climbed the urine stained stairs, the smell catching at his throat, and found the number he was looking for. He wondered if Lisa's story might be better told than seen but he wasn't quick enough. The door opened and a woman carrying a full bin bag fixed her dead eyes on his.

"What do you want?"

It was her voice, but someone had stolen it. It couldn't be Lisa.

"Billy? Christ, Billy – is that you? Look at you, all poshed up. You must be doing well for yourself, eh? It's so good to see you." She patted at her greasy hair, smoothed down the stained shirt and tried to hide the bitten nails by shoving her hands into her pockets. "Wish I'd known you were home. Come on in ... actually, no, don't come in, I've not had time to tidy up. C'mon we'll go for a drink, eh? Catch up on old times? What do you say?"

He wanted to say no. This wasn't his dream, the scene he'd played out in his head all these years.

"Yeah, that sounds nice, Lisa."

"Okay – I'll stick this bag in the bin cupboard on the way out." She started to shut the door behind her.

"Don't you want to get changed? I mean, if we're going for a drink?"

She smiled – the teeth, at least, were still perfect. "Sorry, pet – but this is as good as it gets." She grabbed his arm and held it tight. "I knew you'd come eventually."

He thought he detected a break in her voice, a tear in her eye. He wished he'd never found her, never broken the spell.

In the pub they reminisced, briefly, then she launched into the story of her life. He didn't really want to know, but she was determined to tell him.

"When we moved to Perth I couldn't do anything without my parents' permission – there was no way I could get back to Glasgow to see you. They put a lock on the phone, monitored my calls – it was like being in prison. And then, my mother, the witch – do you know what she did, Billy? She left us. She went away with the local barman. Not the landlord, mind – the barman. He was a total lowlife, only after her money, but she couldn't see it."

The revelation stung Billy in spite of himself. "So, the woman who kept us apart because I wasn't good enough for you, left you and your father for a guy who worked in a pub? You've got to be kidding me?"

"I know – it's mad isn't it? My dad turned to the drink and then gambling. Within eighteen months we were homeless. My hopes of university were gone – my hopes of anything were gone. I came looking for you, Billy, but you'd left. Nobody would give me your address."

Billy's anger at his parents' duplicity surfaced again. He knew Lisa saw it. It was as though she was reading his mind, just like she used to.

"I think your dad would have passed on a message but your mum didn't want to know. She thought it was for the best – that you were happy as you were, that you'd maybe get hurt again. Can't really blame her, I suppose. I'd do the same for mine."

Billy nodded. "So, you've got kids?"

"Aye, four. Can't even afford one, truth be told. But what can you do, eh?" She shrugged and laughed.

Billy tried to smile. You can use contraception, he thought. You can use a bit of sense. "And your husband?"

"Barlinnie. Third time in twelve years. Housebreaking. He's got a habit to feed, so me and the kids go hungry, but at least he's not around much." She clung to his arm. "You'll love the kids, Billy – they're at their aunt's house for the night but you'll meet them soon. They're good kids; I've brought them up well. You'll love them." Her eyes brimmed with tears and desperation. She got up. "I just need to nip to the toilet – I'll be right back."

He sat for a moment and thought about the wasted years and now a wasted journey. What had he expected? Lisa waiting at the airport, her fluffy blonde hair swaying, laughing as she offered him a homemade chocolate turd? He'd lived the dream for so long he'd never contemplated the possibility of a flawed reality. He was in love with a twenty-year-old memory – not this wife of a drug-addicted criminal, mother of four children, remnant of a romantic notion.

He reached into his pocket and took fifty pounds from his wallet. He hesitated then put the money back: better to post it to her – make it a hundred – and add a letter where he'd try to explain things he wasn't quite sure even he understood. He left before the guilt made him change his mind.

In the taxi he thought of all those years he'd blamed the Dentons while his parents were just as bad. If only they'd passed on her messages. And what then? His parents couldn't have put him through university the way his aunt had. He'd probably have ended up in a dump just like the one Lisa called home. Would she have been worth it? Back then he wouldn't have doubted it.

Had he grown hard? Maybe – or maybe he'd just grown up. He'd go back home, tell Ellen he'd lost the plot for a couple of days, blame it on stress at work, make a real go of their life together, maybe even think about starting a family, finally get on with his life and forget about Lisa.

He caught sight of his reflection in the taxi window. There were no traces left of the boy who loved pranks, the boy from the scheme, the boy who loved Lisa Denton. He realised he couldn't hold the new Billy Fairlie's gaze.

Natural Instincts

It was 1976. The year of the big heat-wave, when even Glasgow's tarmac melted. The year of the Montreal Olympics. The year when punk really started. The year when Lorna Garvie died at the high flats just down the hill from St. Brendan's R.C. high school. My school.

We had to walk past the flats at lunchtime, on our way to the bakery on the main street for a bridie and cake. We peered into the close at the Jamieson block where it had happened. There was nothing left to show that it had been a crime scene just four weeks ago. No blood, no torn clothes, no police tape telling us not to cross. Yet I knew we were all thinking the same thing: Lorna Garvie, aged thirteen, raped and murdered by her ex-boyfriend.

I didn't know what was more fascinating: that she'd been murdered, or that she'd had a boyfriend. A boyfriend four years older than her, capable of doing that to her. I wondered if she'd had sex before. When he raped her, was that the first time? What had it felt like?

Some of us had been kissed, a couple had gone a bit further, girls we didn't hang around with had gone all the way, but none of us had been with a boy that much older than us. It didn't seem so cool anymore.

And yet, I couldn't stop thinking about the sex. He had battered her, strangled her, mutilated her and all I could think was that she'd done it – really done it. I'd admitted what I was thinking about to my pals and was relieved to discover they were doing the same.

Angie took charge, as usual. "It's normal to think about that kind of thing. It's normal to be interested in murders and rapes. It's just human nature – we get curious." It was like a speech – Angie didn't talk like that.

Pauline looked at her, eyes wide. "Where the hell did you get that from?"

Angie smiled, flicked her hair back over her shoulder and gave us her latest piece of wisdom. "My dad gets that magazine – you know the one they're advertising on television about famous murders? It comes in twelve weekly parts and you get a special binder to keep it in." She'd learned the advert off by heart.

We nodded.

"Well, it says there's nothing wrong with wanting to find this stuff out, wanting to know the details."

I couldn't believe what I was hearing. "So, the folk that want you to fork out a fortune for their creepy magazine say it's okay to want to know gory murder details? Ach, well, I'm convinced."

Pauline laughed, but Angie hated it when I didn't agree with her.

"See you, Claire, you always do that. You can't stand it when I know more than you about something, can you? You've just got to take the piss."

I shrugged. Secretly I was pleased that some crappy magazine had said we were normal; it was better than nothing.

But I hadn't confessed just how far my imagination went. In my head, I took Lorna Garvie's last walk a dozen times a day. I imagined him grabbing me, me laughing, thinking, 'It's just him – I'm safe enough'. Then realising he's angry; angry 'cause I chucked him. Then he's pinning me against the wall and he's kissing me, rough kissing, forcing. Then his hands are on the outside of my school jumper, feeling all over, then he's pushing the jumper up and he's pulling at my bra. Over his shoulder I can see the big bit of wood we'd all heard about – I try to block that bit out of the dream – then his hands are pulling my skirt up, tugging at my knickers, and then ...

Somebody always interrupted. Probably just as well, 'cause I'd no idea what it would've felt like to have a boy's hands on me like that. And if I went on with the fantasy, where would I stop it? Would I let it go all the way to the end? To Lorna's last breath?

We were silent, Angie in one of her huffs, me in my head, walking in Lorna Garvie's high, white wedges.

"What're you thinking about? You're away in a wee world of your own there." Pauline grabbed my arm, brought me back.

I lied. "Sandy Connolly."

Pauline gave a half sigh, half groan. Sandy, the school heartthrob. Before the murder, he was the main topic of conversation.

"God, I'd just die if he even looked at me," Angie said.

Pauline and I rolled our eyes. Of course he had looked at her; she was the only girl in our year with anything to put in her bra. The only one without plooks. The only one everybody looked at – and she knew it.

Pauline wandered into the dream zone. "Aw, imagine snoggin' Sandy Connolly. Imagine him touching you. If you want to talk about sex, he's the one that gets me really..."

"Sh." I grabbed her arm and pulled her closer. "Sh."

"What is it? Did he hear? Is he coming?"

We were on our way back up the hill, past the flats, past the chapel, past the bus stop and the big, grey proddy school next door to ours, when I saw him.

"Hi Malcolm." I tried, and failed, to sound friendly.

Malcolm kept his head down, muttered, shuffled past – on his own.

Malcolm was Lorna's big brother. He was in fifth year. The boy that murdered Lorna was from the proddy school, but he was Malcolm's best pal. Malcolm had nobody now. No wee sister, no pal, mum and dad too broken up to even know he was there. We felt sorry for him.

"It's a sin for him, isn't it?" Pauline said.

I nodded – a sin, right enough. We looked at Angie and her face went red.

"It's not that much of a sin. I'm still not going out with him – he's an ugly big pig."

"Angie! For God's sake, he's had a terrible time." Pauline was always a wee sweetheart.

"Aye, I know he has. Look, I've said no the last five million times he's asked me out – I'm not changing my mind out of pity. Anyway, he'll not be interested in going out with anybody after what he's been through. Just don't start on me, okay? And anyway..."

"I'm saving myself for big Sandy," we mimicked.

It was good to laugh. Good to be able to laugh.

The teachers – and the priest and the dinner ladies and the cleaners – had treated us all nice for a week or two after Lorna was killed, in case we were dead upset about it. Truth was, Lorna wasn't very popular. All I really knew about her was her and me were the youngest in our year. She was a bit rough – 'a wee hairy' my mum had called her before she died; a wee angel afterwards. But we'd hammed up the pretend grief for all it was worth. The teachers had got wise though, and life was back to normal: crap.

They were piling on the homework, telling us it was just a couple of months 'til the end of term, a couple of weeks until we had to do our options, choose the subjects we'd do in exams, the subjects that would decide 'what we were going to be when we grew up'. Angie had been advised to study science subjects, while I was getting streamed towards languages and the Arts. Pauline had been told to go for Secretarial Studies and Home Economics. Me and Angie were meant to be planning ahead for Uni – Pauline, well, she was meant to get married and work for what our mums called 'pin money.' The future was going to separate us – 'grown-up' was creeping closer.

I wondered what Lorna Garvie would have been. I was sure she had been in remedial English and Maths, so they probably wouldn't even have had her in home eccy or seccy... Then I felt crap for thinking that way: ill of the dead and all that.

But at least we had something to look forward to – the Easter dance was that night. The staff had thought about cancelling because of what happened to Lorna, but changed their minds at the last minute. Apparently it would be just the thing to take our minds off a brutal murder.

It was the first-to-third year dance, but some of the upper school were always roped into helping out – basically making sure nobody was drinking, smoking or trying to snog the face off each other. That was a joke – they were the ones who'd get us the booze, fags and snog us. Angie was in luck; Sandy was on duty. So was Malcolm, which was a shock. I wondered what he was thinking when he saw us all dressed up, dancing, laughing. His wee sister should have been there; was he thinking about her?

No, he was creeping around after Angie.

I was the one who was thinking about her. I was always thinking about her – or at least, what she knew that I didn't. What it really felt like. I had got to the stage where I could get breathless just imagining what Lorna Garvie knew. And that night I wanted to find out. I was so wound up – I had to do something about it. I didn't know how, though; me, Angie and Pauline always stayed together: all for a lumber or all for home.

"Here he comes," Angie whispered. And there he was – Sandy. Strolling towards her. Tall, confident, broad-shouldered, blond hair falling over his blue eyes. He made Angie's night and killed what was left of Malcolm's hopes at the same time.

"Dance?"

It was part request, part instruction. Angie would have taken it any way he wanted to give it. It took me a minute to realise there was someone else there, someone speaking to me.

"Claire? C'mon, don't leave me standin' here like a spare prick."

It was Dougie Nelson. As second best went, Dougie wasn't bad at all. He was brainier than Sandy – not that it would be hard – just as tall but not quite so broad. He was dark –skinned – he took a lot of slagging about that – got hit with every racial slur under the sun. He laughed it off. What else could he do? In a town where your religion was more of an issue than your skin colour, he was getting off pretty lightly. In truth I think the other boys were jealous of – Dougie – all those ginger-haired, pasty-faced North Lanarkshire skinnies would have loved to have a bit of Dougie's colouring and build.

And that night I wanted to be held close, to feel a boy pressed up against me, to know he wanted me. Getting a guy as good looking as Dougie was a bonus.

I was already trembling when he held my hand and took me to the dance floor. And when he held me, God, when he held me, I couldn't believe what it felt like. There were feelings taking over my body I'd only read about in Angie's mum's Harold Robbins books. He was whispering something to me, but 'Please Stay' was playing so loud, I could hardly make out his words.

"... take you home," he was saying

It took me a minute to understand what was going on.

"So, you're asking if you can walk me home?"

He laughed. "Well, yeah, that's the gist of it. What do you say?"

What could I say? I could have said, no – older boys can be dangerous. I should have said, no – I have to stay with my pals. But Angie was snogging Sandy and Pauline was nowhere to be seen. I didn't say anything, I just nodded. I didn't even look back to see if the others had spotted what was going on. I just let him take my hand and lead me out of the door.

As we walked, he chatted about school, his exams, what he planned to do next. He seemed so much older, so experienced. He stopped and he kissed me – not like the couple of kisses I'd had with boys in my year. His tongue was in my mouth and he was pulling me really close to him. And I kissed him back – really kissed him. Let my tongue find his mouth, let my hips push into his, let my nails trail down the back of his head onto his neck. He stopped, looked a bit surprised, smiled, took my hand and we started walking again. I could have walked for miles that night.

But I knew where I wanted to go – where I had to go. So, when he turned the corner at the high flats, the first place that was dry, dark and empty, I led him into the close where it had happened. He didn't complain. I don't think he really registered where I was steering him – just that it was somewhere quiet, a place where anything could happen – if I let it.

There was always a faint smell of pee in the closes of the high flats, so I was glad it was cold and the smell was bearable. Even though it was dark, I could still make out the broken Buckfast bottles and the empty chip wrappers that covered the floor of a place that had seen the end of countless virginities and at least one life. Even in those surroundings, all I could feel was the thrill of what was about to happen.

A moment of sense took over. I wouldn't let it happen. He couldn't think I was easy. He'd never walk me home again if I let him do it on the first date. But then he was pressing me up against the wall – that wall, where she had been. And he was kissing me, and his hands were under my shirt, like I'd imagined, and I could feel that my nipples had gone hard. I could feel that kind of ache and wetness I'd read about. I'd felt it a bit before, when I fantasised, but nothing like this. He was pressing so close – I was shocked to feel how hard he was. So that's what it felt like. I didn't want to stop, didn't think I could.

He took off his jacket, laid it down on the floor and pulled me down on to it. He rolled over on top of me, pushing my skirt up at the same time, the dream coming true with every move.

But I started to imagine it again – just over his shoulder I could picture the piece of wood leaning against the wall. We'd all read about what the rapist had done with that piece of wood after he'd finished with Lorna, after she was dead.

Dougie was still pushing and pulling at me, but I felt cold – a weird feeling, like I wasn't there. He was tugging at my knickers. I felt sick and tears stung my eyes. I let out a sob.

He stopped. "What's up with you? You're not going to try and stop me now, are you?"

I shook my head. "No... it's just that..."

"Fuck's sake – I never took you for a prick-tease. Angie, aye, definitely – but not you, Claire." He whispered the last few words, whispered my name a few more times while he stroked my arm, trying to soothe, trying to get me back to where we had been. Then his hand was under my skirt again, between my legs, pulling my knickers aside, trying to push his fingers into me.

I crossed my legs tight. "I'm sorry – it's just this place. It's Lorna Garvie."

He pulled his hand away, sat up and laughed as he stared at me. "Lorna Garvie? You've got to be fuckin' jokin'. You and your pals had nothing to do with Lorna – and I don't blame you, she was a right wee slag. Most of fifth year reckon they'd had Lorna Garvie."

I didn't believe him. I'd heard all the rumours, believed them all – but that night I just knew they were lies. How many of us had the boys lied about? The tears wouldn't stop. We'd treated her like crap – pretended to care when she died when all we were really interested in was this; what was happening to me. And how could I explain that to Dougie?

I must have looked a mess, tears streaming, mascara running, but he still wasn't ready to give up. He moved onto his side and pressed himself up against me again, kissing my neck, trying to dry my tears with his sleeve. "C'mon, Claire, c'mon, just …"

"She was just a wee lassie." It was all I could think, all I could say.

He stood up so quickly it scared me. He towered over me, making me feel even smaller than I was and for a moment I thought I was going to find out more than I wanted to about what it was like to be Lorna Garvie. He sneered, grabbed his jacket from under me, shook his head, spat his words at me, "Aw fuck this," and left me there.

I lay in the dark, still crying, still seeing a piece of wood that wasn't really there. Still thinking about a girl who was raped and murdered. We were just wee lassies, and no one really cared.

When No One Is Looking

Mrs McLean disappeared when I was the only one watching.

At first she just got smaller and smaller. Never a tall woman to begin with, her clothes hung on her, as though borrowed from an older, big-boned sister. Even her head looked shrunken, hair too full and candy-floss fluffy for the skull it adorned.

I remember trying to tell people.

"Dad, Mrs McLean is tiny."

"Wheesht, Siobhan, I'm listening to the radio." He didn't even look at me when he spoke.

"Mum, Mrs McLean is teeny, tiny, toaty now."

"Away back to reading your book, Siobhan, I'm busy with the cooking." She didn't even take her eyes off the dough she was kneading on the board.

"I've finished my book. But Mrs McLean, she's…"

"You've finished another book? Jesus, that librarian must be sick looking at the pair of us. Well go and play then, but leave poor Mrs McLean alone, do you hear? She's had enough to deal with."

And so she had. I'd heard them talk about all the things she'd lost: her son in a war somewhere far away that Dad said wasn't even our fight; her daughter to a sickness they only ever called the big C; her husband to one of the special hospitals – there were three surrounding our group of villages, so I always thought she'd find him one day if she just looked in the right one – and her sisters and brothers to the four corners of the world. I knew the world was round, but never argued when I ear-wigged on the adults. Then we were all losing Mrs McLean but no one would listen.

One morning I stood at my bedroom window and watched her walk down her garden path. With every step she shrivelled until her clothes dragged along, her head lost inside her cardigan, just the fuzzy hair sticking out of the hole. Then the wind rose and her hair scattered across the grass, like dandelion fluff when I blew it to tell the time, and her shoes stopped walking as her skirt and top crumpled onto them.

Mrs McLean disappeared because I was the only one watching.

Unravelling

This morning I hate you. I wake up, look at you and hate you. You look so innocent, worry lines smoothed out as you lie there. You. Lying.

I stay like that for a while, just staring, hardly breathing. I see your eyelids flutter, the precursor to your morning wide-eyed gaze. You open your eyes, see me watching, give me a smile – a gentle, loving smile – then you look into my eyes and your smile fades; you know it's a hate morning. You lower your gaze, turn away, cuddle up into the duvet, pretending we haven't made contact. You fake sleep-breathing.

I sit, and stare, and hate. When I get up I hear you sigh. Not a sorry sigh to feel me go, a relieved sigh to feel the weight of me leave you.

In the shower I use the exfoliant and the loofah. I scrub until my skin is bright red. It isn't enough. I scrape and scratch, removing invisible traces of you. I work until I bleed. I get out and rub too hard with the towel, wincing, but at least feeling. I pass the mirror – my red, angry reflection. And something else. You. You with the soothing body lotion and forgive-me eyes. I let you apply the lotion, let it sting, let it sink in.

You dress me, slowly, carefully. You dress me 'for the weather'. I let myself go limp, loose, malleable. You steer me to the door, to the real world. At the last moment you put your scarf around my neck. It's too big, too heavy, but I let you wrap it around me.

I wear the scarf all day. It itches and makes me claw at my neck, but I know I can't take it off. It's part of you so I can't hang it on the hook with my old coat. It's there to remind me that you hurt too.

\#

Winter suits you. You, all wrapped up in layers, topped by a huge coat. Me, wanting to unwrap you, to get to the heart of you. Your skin glows in the crisp cold air, your breath is visible, proof that you're alive. I seem to love you more in winter.

But I'm the one who wrapped you up. The one who buried you, so deep. You dig and scratch at yourself while I dig and scratch at the surface of you, hoping to find where you went, where we were, once, a long time ago. I can't have lost you.

It's a hate day – I saw it in your eyes the minute I opened mine this morning. They're becoming more frequent. Your attacks on yourself are increasing. What if I'm not there one day? Will you scrub all the way through to the bone? Is that what you want? I'm never sure who you hate – is it me, or you? Either way, you hurt us both while punishing me.

#

This afternoon I want you. I can't call, can't let you know. I mustn't let you feel wanted on a hate day. I have to get through it, to last a whole day when the tension means swallowing hurts and just breathing in and out takes all I have to give.

You'll ask me to talk. I don't want to talk. I want you to take me, to make me feel something physical, no emotions. But you can't do that – of course, we both know what you are capable of – but not with me. With me it's love and tenderness and looking after. Sometimes it feels more like smothering, like I'm disappearing under the weight of your love.

Is that how you mean it to be? I'm never sure. Are you hoping I'll perform a daring escape or sink so low even you can't reach me?

Your scarf catches on my chair and tightens around my neck. I let it.

#

I imagine you at work, my scarf on the hook, something of me with you. Do you look at it and hate it, too? I want to picture you stroking the wool, feeling for softness and tenderness. Those are the things I'm good at – those are the things I can give to you. I could never be rough with you, never hurt you again.

Sometimes it feels like you want me to hurt you – want me to tighten my grip when we make love. Want me to fuck you, not love you. Sometimes a little of me wants that too. But what if I'm wrong? What if I'm misreading signals? Or inventing signals?

Today I just want to hold you. To comfort you. To let you know I'm sorry for whatever scar you're remembering, whether I inflicted the pain or it was some other lover or friend from the past. I want to make up for us all. I just want to make up.

#

The heat from your scarf has made me uncomfortable all day. Colleagues commented, wondering why I wouldn't take it off. Jokes about love bites. Jokes about double chins and wattle. laughed at them all.

I can still laugh with other people when I hate you. Would that surprise you? I imagine you watching me from across the street, a solitary stake-out in the building opposite, a telescopic lens capturing each mood as it settles on my face for brief moments. A covert collage of my life away from you and my hatred.

Would you be happy knowing that I can fake happiness with others when I can't fake anything with you? I watch the clock, time bleeding away, its trail leading me back to you.

On the train home I decide I won't love you today. Won't forgive you. And tomorrow seems a long way away.

#

I stay at home today and clean the house and prepare dinner. There's no guarantee that you'll eat – sometimes you won't eat for days, just drink glass after glass of water, trying to flush yourself away. Or maybe you're trying to flush away the odium that eats you up and spits me out.

I've washed and ironed any clothes you left in the hamper. The rooms are as clean as one day's work allows. The table is set for our showdown. I watch the door. Your entrance will let me know where I stand or if I should run.

I remember the night you found out about her. The night, so many years ago now, you came home to accuse me. You opened the door so gently, not your usual half-run-half-fall into my arms. I knew.

I hear your keys in the door.

#

I slip into the apartment, start when I see you waiting by the door. The look in your eyes is so desperate, so desolate, it's like you've winded me. I feel my plans crumble to the shining floors.

I turn away from you, take off my coat, hang it on the highest peg, the one I have to stretch for. I slip my shoes off and place them on the mat directly below the hooks. I loosen the scarf, feel my breath release properly for the first time that day, then I walk to you, wind the other half of the scarf around your neck, sit on your knee and let you cry into the wool.

When the weight of the scarf is too much for us both, you lift me up, like I'm a child, and carry me to the bedroom, and I realise I don't want you to hurt me anymore. And I'll stop hurting you – for today, at least.

The Hat

Ian acquired a hat in the hope of acquiring a personality. He stood in front of the mirror, posing the hat with different outfits. Would he need an entirely new wardrobe now that he had a hat, a life? Should his colours be bolder, his cut designer, his price tags pleasingly just beyond his means?

Or maybe this hat could breathe its fabulous fashioned felt into even his saddest beige, polyester, over-washed piece of attire. Should he stop ironing creases in his trousers? Accept that the car coat had seen its day – that its day was March 15th 1973 and it was no longer 'in'?

He pushed the hat to a jaunty angle and became mischievous; his upward glance playful, beckoning. He tilted the brim forward, watched a shadow cover his over-sized nose and magically sculpt it into something more streamlined. He pushed it back, exposing his ears. He shuddered and jiggled it back to jaunty. Jaunty – that was who he had become. Definitely jaunty.

He searched through his wardrobe for something worthy of the hat, but nothing worked. He found his suit. The hat looked uncertain, perched on his head as though it wanted to throw itself onto the bed and weep at its mismatching. The suit joined the pile of rejects on the bed.

The poor light in the basement apartment made his appraisal more difficult. The low ceilings felt oppressive above the hat; it needed more space. He had to go out. But what to wear?

Leaning further into the cupboard, reaching into the darkest corner where only spiders and memories survived, his hands touched leather. That one time, that one week when he was young, before she rejected him, left him shamed in front of the whole class, that one week before he chose to be the geek forever, that week he had worn leather.

Could this be the match for the hat? He had lived with so few excesses Gandhi would probably have told him to get a life, so he knew it would still fit his incongruously youthful frame. The leather felt heavy, he had to straighten his shoulders to take the weight. He felt taller. He threw the hat up, caught it on his head, let it fall where it felt right.

Ian turned and faced the mirror. A stranger peered back. A handsome, confident, mysterious man. The man found his keys, strode out the door and took the stairs to the street two at a time. A blue sky, higher and wider than any he had ever seen, spread above the hat. The man set the hat to its perfect jaunty angle and let it lead him to his fate.

In The Background

It's always her. Everyone who comes to the hospice – consultants, students and now a photographer – is drawn by her grin and her mischief as they clamour to say, "Isn't she just wonderful?"

We're left in the background, unnoticed, too sad, too resigned to our fate. Adele has such spirit, they say. She's such a joker, they say. She's an inspiration to us all.

Well, if I'd reached the age of ninety-four before illness hit me, I'd look a damn sight more cheerful; I could joke, I could inspire. If I had visits from family and friends on a daily basis, if I had every nurse and doctor dancing to my laughter's tune, I could be the bright sun in this wizened world.

Adele will be gone before the rest of us, they say, yet she grins and laughs with a body brimful of happiness. The bitterness inside me sours my breath, twists my belly into hard lumps of loathing, eats me up faster and harder than any disease could.

Lena, always choosing to sit opposite me, revels in my odium. She talks about Adele all the time, loves to watch my face contort with the effort of not responding. Every day she seeks me out. Every day she taunts me with tales of Adele's latest japes and jokes, who loves her most, who is coming to see her today. And the more I shrink into a husk of hate the more Lena's skin glows as she gains strength from my distress.

The photographer is laughing with Adele. Oh, how hilarious, Adele's pretending to photograph the photographer. Why can't I see the humour there? Why am I left here, in the background, prey to my own jealousy – there, I've said it – and Lena's torture. I'm tempted to pull faces, to make rude gestures, to just this once take the attention away from that bloody woman.

Adele turns with a speed and agility that belie her years. For a moment I think she must have read my mind. Is there no end to her talents? She looks at me, she smiles that crumpled smile, her eyes shining under seemingly endless folds of skin. Her voice, so much younger than her mind and body, reaches out to me.

"Geraldine! Come here! You never sit with me, girl. Let the snapper take us both – the prettiest girls in the whole place."

The photographer nods, a nurse claps her hands, everyone stares at me. Lena's eyes narrow and a soft growl escapes her lips.

And I smile. My eyes fill with tears. Adele has noticed me at last. She called me 'girl'. The warmth fills my body and I stand tall, legs shaking, heart jumping as I go to her. And I think, "Isn't she just wonderful?"

Bad Apples

He mixed the paint again, knowing he'd get it right eventually. It shouldn't be so problematic; it was just a still life. People were difficult, so they said, but not for him. He could paint a person (he never used the word 'portrait') and show their whole lives in the tilt of a head, the crook of an arm, the slump of a shoulder.

People were easy. While other artists starved, his work was sought after, commissioned, offers of patronage, and other, more interesting offers from female clients, came daily.

He started again. The table was perfect; it looked well used, well cared for, a table that had been loved. The bowl was beautiful; he'd brought out the craftsmanship. It was no ordinary bowl; it represented the art of the potter. It represented art itself.

He dipped his brush into green and daubed, once more, at the troublesome shapes in the centre of the canvas.

Defeated, he threw his brush across the studio. It was no good; the bloody things still just looked like apples.

Here Lies Truth

I remember every lie I've ever told. They replay in my head like an old 8mm home movie: flickering frames rolling in a continuous loop. The images seem to leak from my mind into my bloodstream, leaving an acrid taste in my mouth and bitter secrets in my heart.

It's time to make them stop.

#

My name is Richard, but everyone calls me Ricky. I'm 10 years old. Dad died last month. Sudden heart attack. I don't get it. Dad was really fit, always out playing football, swimming, running. He played with me all the time. How can someone just die when they're not even that old?

At least I've still got Mum.

#

I walk through the nettle and bramble scented lanes of childhood, breathing in the remnants of past innocence, future horror, present contentment. If I close my eyes I can hear the chimes of the ice-cream van, the calls of 'Goal!' the chants that accompany the beat of the skipping ropes. I have had so many years to enhance my imaginative senses, years buried in books, searching for answers – sometimes I think it would be better to stay isolated; how can reality ever live up to memory and nostalgia?

The locals skirt around me, as if I was four feet wide and taking up the whole pavement. They clutch their bags, their children, their friends closer avoiding my notional, personal space. They don't recognise me: how could they? But something tells them to stay away. They should listen to those voices in their heads – they always speak the truth. Justified paranoia is always denied – let it breathe, let it spread, let it save your life – nothing else will.

#

My name is Richard, but he calls me Dick – he makes it sound nasty. I'm 11 years old. He's Mum's boyfriend. He hates it that I'm clever; tries to take my books away, but they're my only escape. I'm supposed to call him Uncle Ian, but I don't use uncle with my real relatives, so why should I use it with him? He's teaching me why. He teaches Mum lessons, too. He teaches her lessons about the right way to make his sandwiches, the right way to make the bed. I get nightmares about the ironing lesson. The hissing sound, the burning smell ...

My friends' mums have started acting funny with me. They whisper to each other when they think I'm not watching. They pat my head a lot, find excuses to give me hugs, kiss me goodbye the same way they do with their own kids. It's weird. I wish they'd stop. I've got my own mum for that. She still does it when Ian's not around. She's still Mum. She still loves me.

I tell them everything at home is fine, what a great laugh Ian is, how happy Mum is.

#

I have perfected my counterfeit emotions so that no one could question their authenticity. I can live among these people as if I was one of them. That is what I plan to do. They won't know why they doubt me, why they are apprehensive – until it's too late. They will convince themselves that they are the ones with the problem; that they have an unnatural fear of strangers. But I am no stranger – not exactly an old friend, but certainly a familiar name. Eventually they will remember.

#

My name is Richard. I'm 12 years old. My teachers call me Richard. They are worried about my grades. I've always been top of the class at everything. They want to know why my work is so bad. Am I still upset because of Dad's death? If that's the problem they'll understand, get me extra classes and something called 'grief counselling.' I tell them I'm fine. I hardly think about Dad. I've got a new dad now. They nod.

"And how are you getting on with your step-father."

"Great. He's great. I'm sorry about my grades. I'll work harder."

"How did you get that bruise on your cheek?"

"Oh, that was one of the other boys. We were having a laugh on the bus and it got out of control – I hit my face off someone's shoe."

"Richard, is someone bullying you?"

"Bullying? No, 'course not. I'd tell you if there was anything like that going on."

They believe me.

"You've always been a great student, always working hard, always lost in one of your books – we have to find out why that's changing. Should we talk to your mum and step-dad?"

"No, it'll be fine. And please don't call him my step-dad – he's my dad now."

I hear my words, hear my lies, hear their acceptance as though I'm watching a school play.

#

My old house has recently been vacated by the last in a long line of tenants. I walk up the path, finding it difficult to control the tremble that threatens to over-rule my composure. Shadows appear at the windows of the houses on either side. I stop, turn slowly towards number 27 and stare at the window until the curtain slowly falls from the wrinkled hand of Mrs Jenkins. She's still there: good. I turn to number 23 and repeat my challenge. The man stares back, defiant, cocky even. A look of fear crosses his face and he steps back unsteadily, the curtain flailing, as I know his memory will be. He'll try to place me, but he won't believe it. Logic will convince him of his error.

It's going to be easier than I expected.

#

My name is Richard. I'm 13 years old. My foster parents call me pet. At first I thought they were a little afraid of me. I thought that was funny. Having spent so much time living in terror, living with lies, living with Ian – that someone should be afraid of me was weird. There was a strange power in that idea. I could see how causing fear could feel good.

But I was wrong: they don't fear me. Their gentle voices and careful questions are a sign of how much they care, how much they want to help. It reminds me of life before Dad died. Now there is someone to ask me about school, to help me with homework, to hold me when the nightmares come.

I wish I could stay here.

Mum's funeral was pretty grim. The whole village turned out, of course, but none of them could look at me. I felt their knowledge of my guilt hang like an extra cloud over the open grave.

Ian's body won't be cremated until the police have finished with it. I hope they don't lock me up before I get to see him burn.

#

I turn the key in the lock to my old/new home and step over the threshold of apprehension into the miasma of memories that almost suffocate me as the door closes gently behind me.

A hint of Mum's Youth Dew caresses my nostrils, Dad's trainers lie at the foot of the stairs, a television programme entertains the furniture as I drop my schoolbag on the couch and run through to the kitchen. Mum and Dad are making dinner together, chatting, laughing, ignorant of his impending death.

"Hey, Ricky! How was school?" Dad stops chopping onion and smiles at me, waiting to hear about my day.

I shake away that image, brush away the tears, gulp a breath of reality into my lungs.

Another memory is lying in wait to assault my sanity. Another day, another homecoming, another smell.

#

My name is … does it matter? Nothing seems real anymore. Names, ages, innocence, guilt – they seem to have slipped into a void where nothing makes sense.

I watched him burn.

Only a couple of the locals attended that time; 'ghouls' the social worker called them.

I cried. I didn't cry at Mum's funeral, but I cried like I wouldn't ever stop at his cremation.

Social worker and doctor said it was okay; it was normal. Normal?

I was in shock, they say. Shocked that my step-father killed my mother, shocked that he tried to kill himself, shocked that by pulling the knife out I couldn't save him.

They know I feel guilty about trying to save him even though he beat us both, but I was just a kid; I should stop being so hard on myself.

The inquest called it a murder and a suicide. No one to blame. I fell apart then, ended up in this place. Not free, not happy, but safe.

#

The new smell is unmistakable: blood. I can hear that whimper; an entreaty without words. I try to stop my mind from going back into that kitchen, from seeing her lying in the blood that poured from her neck, from seeing him with the knife sticking out of his chest, his hands reaching out to me for help as his failure to die gives way to a desire to live.

I feel the nausea rise as the film in my head rolls on to the next scene, the one where I reach for the knife, the one where he smiles as he thinks I'm going to help him, the one where his eyes bulge with shock as I twist, twist, twist that knife before I pull it out.

I slide down the wall and bury my head between my knees, just like I did that day. Except this time there is no knife in my hand – only the keys to the past and the future.

#

My name is Richard, but everyone calls me Ricky. I'm 28 years old. I've gone through years of therapy since the death of my mother. It has taken many years and many attempts on my own life for them to convince me that I was not to blame.

I thought that I had killed her with my lies; that if I'd told people the truth about Ian they would have helped, they would have saved us – that I could have saved her.

I know now that it wasn't my fault, that I was a child caught up in a terrible, impossible situation. My lies were not the problem. I was not the problem. Now they say I can go back out into the world, into the community; now I can start to live again.

I am innocent. I am at peace with myself and the world. I am a danger to no one – especially not myself.

#

As I sit on the floor I blame them all. All those adults – the teachers, neighbours, friends' mums – they knew. They saw the fear in my eyes, the change in my behaviour. They saw the bruises and the cuts. They knew my mother, they knew me, they knew something was wrong.

They did nothing. They accepted my excuses with sighs of relief. Relief that they wouldn't have to become involved. How convenient for them that we disappeared from their lives.

But I am back where I belong. I'm strong now. I won't move from this place again. I'll walk the streets of this quiet, unchanged village, walk among them every day until they realise who I am. I'll look them in the eyes, accuse them with my stares, condemn them with my silence.

The guilt will rise like bile in their throats and they'll choke back apologies, platitudes and excuses. I swear that they'll have no peace. It's time to bury the lies.

It's good to be home.

Merging

He looks far too comfortable on that couch.

"It's like we don't 'gel', you know what I mean? Like there's nothing tangible connecting us," he says.

I nod, looking at my watch, wishing this session was over.

"It's like she doesn't get me, you know?"

I raise one eyebrow, an unspoken 'carry on', while I try to stop my teeth grinding so hard it'll be audible.

"It's like, we're together, you know – I mean, we are together – but we're separate, you know what I mean?"

I write 'get me the fuck out of here' on my pad, but cock my head to one side in an understanding way.

"It's like, we don't merge, you know. Yeah, that's it – we never, ever seem to like, merge, you know?"

I put down my pen, steeple my fingers and tap them against my chin, fake pondering. I have this image of merging him and her with the help of a giant wood chipper. The image is pleasing. I smile.

"Hah – you get it, don't you, Doc? See, she doesn't get me – she wouldn't get the merging idea. But you get it. You get me."

I look at my watch. "I'm afraid that's all we have time for this week." I imagine getting him. Getting him and slapping my clipboard off his slack-jawed face.

He gets up, stretches his toned body so that I can see his tanned, tight abs. I know he has platinum credit cards in the pocket of his designer jeans. I know those highlights came care of the most expensive, though not necessarily the best, hairdresser in the city. I know his Porsche is parked outside – probably in the disabled bay.

Yep, he has a lot to worry about. My heart bleeds for him.

"Thanks, Doc. Same time next week?"

I stand, shake his moist hand. "Of course. I'll look forward to seeing you."

I watch his lazy, slouched-walk. Not a care in the world now he's dumped them all on me. I press the intercom and call in the next whining bag of shit. They're all the same – too much money, too few real problems.

I no longer see them as individuals. It's like they've, you know, just merged.

Awkward Hearts

From half way up the hill, the rain looks like a heavy curtain over the car park, almost making it disappear. I don't want to go back down, back to my son's sympathetic eyes, his wife's soft voice, the tense smiles like fault lines on their strained faces. I didn't want to come here at all, but if I had to, I wanted it to be alone. No – not allowed. I have to be watched now, as though I might evaporate if they stop looking.

Eat this, don't drink that, wrap up warm. Jesus Christ – you'd think I was a child. A helpless, useless child. So what if I'm quieter now, am lost in thought at times, don't smile so much? I miss her. What do they want from me, hysterics? That's not my way and it never was. She hated people who made a fuss. We were never dramatic; it was one of the things that bound us together as a couple, our stoicism. They should know that.

I didn't want to scatter her ashes. I wanted to keep them. Nope – that's weird. The tree was their idea, where everyone in the whole bloody town has carved their name over the years. It's no more special for us than it is for anyone else, for them. I didn't argue. There's no point in arguing anymore. When I try to say how I feel, what I want, their heads tilt so far to the side I'm afraid they'll fall over. So today I trudge further up the hill, getting drenched – even they hadn't foreseen this storm – hugging the urn that holds what's left of her. Dust. She hated dust.

My heart flutters. Hearts. It always comes back to hearts. Hearts on the tree. Her heart. Her awkward heart that refused to respond to treatment. I run my hands over the shapes carved in the bark – broken by time, all of them.

When I'm sure no one can see me, I take the empty sandwich bag from my pocket, shelter under the tree and decant the contents of the urn. I seal the bag tight and put it in my pocket. A giggle gurgles in my throat and I have to swallow hard to keep it from escaping. Must look suitably somber when I get back down there. But this is the first time I've felt alive since she went.

I tuck the empty urn under my arm, shove my hands in to my pockets and head back down the hill. I let my fingers close around the soft bag. I'll keep her with me and she'll help me heal. And one day, I'll be able to say her name again.

All the Fun

At the back of the Blackpool Pleasure Beach there used to be a huge building with massive, crooked red letters proclaiming that this was the FUN HOUSE. A Fun House. A house just so full of fun it said so right above the door.

When I was a child, our family holidays meant Blackpool, and for me and my three older brothers, Blackpool meant the Pleasure Beach. However, Dad was always reluctant to let us explore the Fun House. We couldn't think why. Was it the extra admission fee? Or was it viewing the outside passageway where you could see people walk across, let out a sudden scream and then briefly disappear?

The passageway may have served as a warning to Dad but to us it was an enticement. Why were they screaming? What was going on? What were we missing out there, with our candyfloss and doomed goldfish we had won by first terrifying as we threw hoops over their bowls?

Eventually our pleading and whining wore Dad down. He grumbled as he paid the entrance fee but we assured him it would be worth it. After all, now we had access to – well, whatever was going to be so much fun.

The fun started the minute we went through the door. We had to negotiate three sets of six-feet-high skittles, which were rigged to bang together at imprecise intervals. The trick was to time it right and run through. It was a trick I never mastered.

The skittles were plastic but seemed to have been reinforced with steel. No matter how hard I tried, no matter how many times Dad's face appeared through the gaps to safety, the skittles clattered me to and fro until I fell out the other side, battered, bruised, but determined not to cry. It was our holiday, and Dad never tired of telling us, "Yous are here tae enjoy yersels." And

71

anyway, Mum promised to buy me a pokey-hat to take my mind off the pain.

Having passed the first test, we thought we were into the main attractions. Not so simple. Next we found out why people had been screaming and disappearing from that outside passageway. The cold evening air hit us and we discovered that the floor leading back inside consisted of square, steel sections. Step on the wrong section and your foot plunged into what felt like oblivion but was really just a dip – but a dip big enough to break an ankle. Dad carried me through successfully. My three brothers ran through with the kind of mad abandon that makes me glad they've never been in a situation where they had to negotiate a minefield.

Once inside, the possibilities for bruising, bleeding and maiming were endless. If Pennywise had a holiday home, it would have been The Fun House. But I had my cone and I was happy. I opted for a go in a strangely hypnotic spinning barrel. The point was to get inside and run – run your little legs off in time with the barrel's spin. If you didn't ... well, if you didn't, you ended up like me. I got in and ran – next thing I knew I was hitting the floor of the barrel, being spun to the top and then dropped in a heap, spun to the top, dropped in a heap, spun to the top – yeah, you get the picture.

I had been badly sun-burned that day (it was the 60s so sun cream meant being basted with pure coconut oil and sent out to broil to a ripe tomato redness) and the sun-burned skin was being methodically ripped from my exposed arms and legs, but the ice-cream from the cone was landing on me with every revolution of the barrel, providing a soothing but ultimately unsatisfying balm. Mum and Dad were screaming at the two big boys who'd climbed in either side of me to let me out, Dad repeating "Bloody hell!" over and over again. The boys weren't bad, they just couldn't let me out because they didn't know how get off the stupid thing either. Dad assisted. One boy was grabbed by the scruff of the neck and deposited in a grateful heap at Dad's feet. Then Dad reached in for me and was almost sucked into the vortex of fun I was having. But he was a big guy and no bloody spinning barrel was going to get the better of him.

Safe in Mum's arms, what was left of my arms was covered in Pond's Cold Cream and kisses. Dad decided it was time to find my brothers and get out of the place.

We found one brother trapped and crying at another 'attraction'. This particular instrument of torture was really quite ingenious. Two steel chutes facing each other, meeting in a steel valley. The idea was to run as fast as you could down the first chute, thus building up sufficient momentum to make your way up the second. Many small children, like my brother, couldn't do it. Those whose parents hadn't accompanied them into the Fun House may have been stuck there for years, like those prisoners of war who didn't know it was all over, waiting for rescue and, in this case, a cone to soothe their pain.

But we had Dad and his now familiar mantra of, "Bloody hell!" He climbed the stairs, hurtled down the first chute, grabbed my brother's T-shirt and hauled him up the second chute, reaching the top with a gasp that could have heralded a heart attack, but was really just a precursor to another, "Bloody Hell!"

Two more brothers to find and we could mount our escape. When we heard screams coming from across the room we knew where to go.

The oldest brothers were on 'The Record', a steel disc with a pole in the middle (seriously, these people must have had shares in a steel works). The disc spun at a ridiculous speed. One person ran on and held onto the pole, everyone else ran on and held on to that person. About sixty kids were now pinning their hope of remaining on the disc on clinging to one v-neck jumper – my brother's jumper. Nobody's knitting's that good.

Children were being hurled off and smacking the walls at a rate of three per second, Dad valiantly trying to gather them all up and deliver them to shocked parents. When my brothers were eventually thrown free of the contraption, Dad said, "Right, let's get out of this bloody place."

We didn't want to go. There were things we hadn't been on yet. There was the zip wire, the biggest chute in the world, the...

Dad gave us a look that said, 'Move!' We moved. Well, we limped, we dragged, we whimpered.

Back in what now appeared to be the sanity of the main Pleasure Beach, our cries of, "Can we get waffles? Can we, Dad? Can we get waffles?" were met with a stony stare of disbelief from Dad and a gentle, "Let's go," from Mum.

The fun was over. Well, until next year. The Fun House would probably have been filled with new ways to kill us by then. And we couldn't wait.

Shells

George wore the big, tweed coat on egg-stealing days. When he got to the supermarket he took off his woolly hat and put it in his pocket, creating a cosy nest. He checked the bread and egg aisle for other shoppers. Safely alone, he took a free-range egg and slipped it on top of the hat. He only took one egg per week; he knew he could steal one each day, with a break on the Sabbath, and have a full half-dozen, but that would be taking too much, crossing a moral line that only he could see.

He made his way to the checkout, casual, no hint of panic, no fear of being caught. He laid his goods on the conveyor – the tinned salmon was an extravagance, he always bought something he didn't need on egg-stealing day – and smiled at the checkout girl. The girl with the pierced lip today. He smiled at her so she would smile back and he could see her lips stretch and wait for the stud to come flying out. One day it would, he was sure. He packed his shopping into his 'bag for life' and walked home.

The Blue Hills housing complex was just across the road from the shop. He wondered who had come up with the name; there were no hills in sight, blue or otherwise. Still, it was handy for the shops, and the bungalow saved wear and tear on the joints – he couldn't argue with his son's logic. Not like the old place. So many stairs, rooms with ceilings so high he got vertigo painting them. The old garden, with the roses he had tended over forty years, had become such a trial, he agreed.

"You're too old for this place, Dad. Mum's health is getting worse; you're having to do more and more for her, more up and down those stairs every day. You can't keep going like this. You need to get a smaller place – somewhere safe."

"I could move her bed downstairs – that would make it easier for both of us. She'd like that – she'd be able to see the garden better."

"She'd hate that! She'd feel like an exhibit, on display for everyone who comes to visit whether she likes it or not. And she loves her sitting room, loves how she decorated it. No, she'd hate to have her bed down here."

"Really, Kenny? More than she'd hate not being here at all?"

"You have to face facts, Dad – it's time to move on."

But he missed climbing, missed his roses, missed the tiny triumphs.

He walked across the patch of lawn with the 'Keep off the Grass' sign, swivelling his feet slightly with every step, and up to the front door of the tiny house. Once inside, he unpacked his bag, keeping the salmon aside for the cat, then took the egg from his pocket and threw it in the bin.

He walked the few steps to the bedroom and looked in on Betty. Still asleep. She slept a lot. Life was easier when she slept, easier to drag his way through the day. Just him and the cat and relative silence while Betty slept. He felt guilty when he thought that way, but asleep she was calm, pain-free.

He looked out at the garden. A tiny patch of green to call his own. He never did anything with it – it hardly seemed worth the effort. It was fine for a clothes line, but no space for anything more. It had its uses. That was what the whole place was about – being functional and safe. Somewhere they'd have help on hand if either of them fell (ill or over – he was never sure which), somewhere close to the health centre, somewhere easy to manage, just like him.

"It's perfect, Dad. You and Mum will love it here."

"Perfect? Well, it's small, right enough."

"But that's just it – so easy to clean, no long walks upstairs to feed Mum, to take care of her. Everything on hand."

"It certainly is – if I turned round in that kitchen I'd be cleaning the units with my backside."

"Don't exaggerate."

"No. No, this is not for us – there's no garden to speak of. She likes a garden."

"She can't get out to the bloody garden anymore!"

"No, but she can see from the window – she's not blind, you know. And if you're that concerned about her, why don't you come over more, eh? Bring Jill and the kids?"

"You're changing the subject. You know I'm right. And anyway, what's the point in having all your money tied up in the old house, eh? You never know when you might need it – for Mum's care, eh? Trust me, this is best for everyone."

He should have fought, should have held out for a bungalow – or even a flat – by the sea. The money from the old house would have covered that and plenty to spare. But not enough. Not enough for Kenny. Kenny told Betty what a great community they'd join at Blue Hills. Not isolated in some seaside town that was wonderful in summer but would cause her more pain in winter. Yep, a great community of creeping cancer and cardiac arrest. Kenny could do no wrong, no matter how much evidence to the contrary mounted up over the years. Betty saw only good in their son. He wished he could still see even a little of that boy, the one Betty had never lost sight of.

"What do you mean, we won't be seeing them anymore? What the hell are you talking about?"

"She left me, took the kids, doesn't want any contact."

"What, not even with us? It'll break your mother's heart."

"Thanks. Thanks for caring about how I'm feeling, by the way."

"Sorry – it's just a shock. Of course I care. If there's anything I can do …"

"Look, I need cash. If I can pay off the debts, she might give me another chance. And you've got the money from the house – you're not doing anything with it. It could save me."

"Money, eh? And when exactly did Jill leave you?"

"Does it matter?"

Betty's condition deteriorated after they sold the house – losing the familiar, losing the comfort. She slept through the packing and the sorting. She slept away most of the day to day grind. She was lucky. Sleep eluded him. Interminable crosswords and sudoku to keep his brain active, to fend off Alzheimer's, meant he was constantly alert.

She'd be awake soon. He warmed the pot and put Betty's favourite tea next to her favourite cup, on her favourite tray.

He tickled Casper under the chin. "Hey, Casper – let's get away from here. Let's go somewhere we've never been before. I fancy some colour in my life – how about you? Let's just pack up our stuff, me, you and Betty, and run away."

Casper arched his back, disdaining the caress, hopped up onto the kitchen unit and looked at the tin of salmon. Pink salmon. At least Casper would have some colour.

"George! George! Are you there?"

George sighed. "Yeah – be through in a minute. Just feeding the cat."

He took the tin opener and pierced the tin, Casper's purrs increasing with every twist of the handle.

"Is Kenny here?"

"Not yet."

"But it's Tuesday – he never misses his Tuesday visit."

George scraped the salmon into the bowl. Casper accepted the offering without a look or purr of thanks. Cats and weans, ungrateful, selfish gits.

"Lost it all? What do you mean, lost it all?"

"For fuck's sake – do you have to question everything? Lost it, gambled it. Same as I did with the first lot. There, are you happier now that you know?"

"So that's why Jill…"

"Yeah, rub it in, rub it right in – as if it doesn't hurt enough to know what a waster I am."

"Aye, you must be in terrible pain."

George helped Betty sit up, plumped pillows to support her, combed her hair, helped her with her teeth, washed her hands and face, applied her creams and eased her into her bed-jacket.

"I'll get you some toast and tea."

"Did he call? Is he coming?"

"Yes, of course."

He watched her mouth purse, her eyes squeeze together as a wave of pain hit her. He hugged her, gently. "Are you well enough today? Should I ask him to come tomorrow?"

"Oh, tomorrow's no good. He has meetings on Wednesdays."

George bit his bottom lip. "Yes, of course he does." Kenny could meet with his bookies any day.

"Don't tell her, eh? She's got enough to suffer. Please, Dad – never tell."

The front door opened. "Dad? Mum? Anybody in?"

George clenched his jaw. Where else would they be? "Aye, we're through here, in the bedroom."

Kenny walked past him and hugged Betty, too tight, George could see it was too tight, but she waved him away when he moved to help. He backed off, leaving them to their embrace.

"I'll get you a cup of tea while I'm making some for your mum."

"Any chance of something to eat, Dad? Do me one of your special omelettes, eh?"

George allowed himself a smile. "Sorry – no eggs."

It wasn't much, but it was better than nothing.

Colouring In

Everything has to be purple. I've got the streaks in my hair, the right shade of eye-shadow, the most perfect lipstick. Clothes are easy – if I can't find the colour I want, I dye them. I've ended up with some of the coolest tie-dye stuff; okay, the tie-dying was an accident, but it looks fantastic.

At school, they look at me like I'm weird. Someone asked if I was going to a fancy dress party. Who are they to talk, with their brown shirts and blue trousers, with their green blouses, faded jeans and stupid, sparkly high heels? They think I look weird? They should take a look in a mirror sometime. The things they think 'go together' just don't. They look like they fell into a pile of clothes and came up wearing anything that stuck.

'Purple Patty': that's what they call me now. It's better than 'Cow Pat', my old nickname, the one the teachers insisted was 'affectionate'.

I've bought purple-tinted shades so I can look at my classmates without wanting to throw up.

#

My stomach aches. I saw these plums in the shop and they were so beautiful, so purple, I bought two punnets. I wasn't going to eat them; I just wanted to look at them, to have them in my room. But then I thought about how awful it would be when they rotted away, went brown and got fuzzy mould-beards.

I ate one, planning to eat one a day until they were gone. My teeth sank into the flesh and a teardrop of juice dripped onto the duvet cover. It fanned out, kind of like a kaleidoscope, but just the one colour – just purple and perfect. I let a few more drops fall and make a pattern.

The other plums looked sad without the plum I had stolen, so I had to eat them all, to send them all to the same place. I thought they'd be happier together, but they've made my stomach hurt, so I must have got that wrong.

I do get it wrong sometimes, especially with purple. It's not an easy colour. It can be quite demanding, cruel, petulant. Like now. Hurting my stomach. I like the word 'petulant', it makes me think of petals – purple petals.

I took some of Dad's indigestion medicine. It's pink, but with a little food colouring added to each dose, it turns out quite a nice shade of purple. Soothing, like it should be. I keep the medicine bottle in my box of Dad's things – things I knew Mum wouldn't miss. I'm painting and dyeing everything in my box of purple memories.

#

My art teacher got angry with me today. Said I have to use more colours. I did use different shades, but that wasn't good enough. I tried to use some pink and some blue, but my hand shook so violently, they merged with the purple and blended in. It's what the colours wanted; they wanted to be purple. Miss Ruddy didn't understand. I was sent to the headmaster's office for being 'insolent.'

Insolent sounds like a purple thing to be, so I agreed I had been insolent but that I hadn't meant to be and promised not to be insolent in Miss Ruddy's class in the future.

I don't like her name – it's reddy-brown. I hate red. It's my least favourite colour. Maybe that's why I'm insolently purple in her class. Our colours clash. I won't go to her class anymore, now that I've promised not to be insolent.

#

I was lying on my bed, listening to music, when Mum came in and started shouting at me. Why was I making life so difficult for her? Didn't I realise what she had been through, how hard it was to get on with things after Dad died? She was getting calls from school about my work and my behaviour.

She slumped down on the bed and started crying and hugging me. Saying sorry over and over again. She was being insensitive, it was harder for me, she knew that. I was the one who'd found him, how could he have done that to me? Poor Patty, my poor, poor Patty. Over and over, rocking me back and forth. Poor, poor Patty.

She got a tissue and wiped my eyes (I hadn't been crying). Would I like to go back to the man I talked to after it happened? She never says psychiatrist; don't know why, I think it's a good word. I said I didn't need to talk, everything was fine, just needed to be left on my own for a while, work things through (I'd heard that on 'Tricia', it sounded like the right thing to say to Mum).

It worked. She nodded, patted my arm, said she'd talk to the school and try to get me some leeway. I asked if I could skip art classes, said they reminded me of Dad because he used to love my paintings. She looked surprised. Well, it wasn't true; she and I both knew Dad never took any interest in my school work, but she wasn't going to argue with me.

She nodded, promised to phone the headmaster and then left. I was so relieved. Those green trousers had hurt my chest; I couldn't breathe with them sitting on my bed. Those red arms wrapped round me felt like they were burning my back and my shoulders. Red really hurts. Red is lethal.

I slid under my duvet and closed my eyes. I saw his face, on the back of my eyelids. Bloated, eyes bulging, tongue lolling. And his skin, so purple.

#

I've been expelled from school. Mum was really upset. She phoned the psychiatrist. I have to go and stay at the hospital where he works. Just for a while, she said. The police will talk to me again when I'm settled. Mum packed a case for me, but I wanted my purple bag, so I emptied everything out onto the floor.

I know she wanted to shout at me, but she was frightened I'd go nuts again. That's what they told her – I'd lost the plot and attacked another pupil. I didn't lose anything. I knew exactly what I was doing. I didn't have my tinted glasses on when I saw her sitting in the cafeteria, the one who'd started calling me 'Putrid Patty', my latest 'affectionate nickname', and I saw red. I felt she'd look better if her face was covered in purple bruises. Sometimes you just know these things. The colours tell you. So I punched her. I kept punching until they pulled me off.

I take after my dad, you see. He knew all about the effects and powers of colours. He used to have black moods, grey days, felt blue. All the letters with the red writing, those were what made his mood black, his days grey, his mood blue. It was red that made him do it.

That day I found him in the kitchen he looked so surprised, like the purple had surprised him. It'll never surprise me. I've got it under control. I've got almost all the colours under control. Except red.

Curiosity

She had a grape in her hair. He wasn't sure if it was supposed to be there – some sort of affectation. He wondered if he should mention it, just walk up and say, "Excuse me, but do you know you have a grape in your hair?"

Well, it would be awkward, wouldn't it? If she didn't know, she would be embarrassed, would feel compelled to find and provide an explanation. Maybe she'd enlist his aid in grape retrieval. He really didn't want to get involved with a stranger's hair.

And if she did know it was there, he didn't want to get involved with any part of a woman who deliberately kept a grape in her hair. She caught him staring. "Hey, are you looking at my grape?"

He nodded, guiltily.

"Well, don't. A face like yours could bruise it."

He lowered his head, swallowed the obvious question: "You have red hair – why are you sporting a green grape?"

Sometimes, he decided, it's best not to ask.

If The Wind Changes

When I heard Mum's voice on the phone last night it winded me. I thought he must have died, could think of no other reason for her to make contact.

"I'm sorry to bother you, I know you're awful busy, but your dad's had a stroke and I think it might be a good idea for you to come …" – she won't say the word, won't give me an inch – "…for you to visit him."

I hadn't realised I'd missed her. I had to gulp away tears, not just because of the news about Dad, but hearing her voice, softer because she was talking on the phone, but still strong, still Mum.

Growing up, our house held no secrets from the rest of the street, our mother's voice made sure of that. She was an equal-opportunities yeller; good news and bad ricocheted off the walls before bouncing out the windows – always open for the fresh air, unless there was fear of actual flooding from a storm of horizontal rain – and into the small world outside.

Our father blamed her loudness on her work. All those years shouting over the noise of vacuum cleaners when she and the other women put the local cinema back to pristine condition after each screening. All those school lunches prepared in kitchens where industrial mixers and clattering pot lids tried and failed to stop the workers gossiping as they earned their living. She lost the ability to speak any other way. Her voice – as she threatened would happen to our huffy faces if the wind changed – stayed that way forever.

Ever the quiet man, my father resembled a mime act in her presence, becoming quieter and quieter until his vocabulary shrank to the occasional grunt with all other communication made through points, shrugs, and nods and shakes of his head. If she noticed his disappearing act, she never commented.

My brothers and I grew into quiet children who had learned that competing with Mother was futile. We inherited our father's low register and quiet nature and so became something of a mystery to our mother. We liked it that way. It was our father who knew what really happened in our lives. Since an accident at work left him disabled, he was the one always at home, always there for us. He passed on our worries, our fears, our moments of happiness to our mother – presumably he chose a time of day when her mouth was full of food – and she passed our lives on to the rest of the street via the open windows.

I couldn't walk to school without my neighbours commenting on every tiny detail of my life.

"Congratulations on your exam results, Eilidh!"

"Sorry to hear you didn't get the part in the school play, Eilidh!"

"Hope that rash clears up soon, pet!"

And I hated it. I hated our little house, the narrow street, the village, the neighbouring villages. I hated that everyone knew everything about my life. I hated it all and plotted an escape.

I'd become a famous actress, move to Hollywood. Not getting a part in the school play should have alerted me to the implausibility of this particular dream, but I shoved negative thoughts out of my mind. I'd become a famous tennis player – even though I'd never so much as held a tennis racquet in my life – and move to Australia. I'd become a famous author – even though English was never my best subject – and live in Paris.

My father pointed out the biggest flaw in my plans. "The people who know you here, who know your life, are people who care about you, who'll look out for you. If you became some big famous actress, or sports star, or author, the people who'd write about you would write lies to sell their papers. The people who'd pretend to care would only do it for money. I know you hate it now, but one day you'll see that this place is not so bad."

I snorted, stomped out of the room, long hair flying behind me like a veil.

"But keep that up and you'll maybe at least get into the next school play – it'd be a start, eh?"

He knew I'd laugh, but he also knew I wouldn't do it until I'd shut the bedroom door and he couldn't hear me. Mum would never have known that about me.

What he didn't say – what no one talked about – was that as the youngest, the last one left at home, I'd be expected to stay, to help out, to sacrifice my life to their old age. It never needed to be said, it was just how things were supposed to be. My path was clear to them: I'd get a job in a nearby town, live with Mum and Dad and contribute to household expenses until my inevitable marriage when I'd find my own home in the village, still close, still available.

When I announced my intention to not only leave the village, but leave the country and attend university in England, reactions were as expected. Dad was partly proud, I knew he was, but he couldn't hide the sadness at losing me to a life he never thought I'd want. It was fine for the others, but not for me, not for his little girl. Mum went quiet. I think it's the only time I have, or probably will, ever use that sentence regarding my mother. She looked confused, then the anger built and the shouting started.

Yes, I was well aware that since Dad's accident she was the only one working – it was the only family life I'd ever known. Yes, I knew my brothers and their families were scattered around Britain and that she would be left to do everything, as well as work two jobs. Yes, I bloody well did think it was fair.

"What?"

"Yes. Yes, I think it's fair. You took vows. You said, 'In sickness and in health.' This was your choice – it's not mine."

The arrogance of youth – I can see that now. And I can see the thing I've never been able to erase from my memory. I see the wounded look in Dad's eyes. I see him try to shake it away, to smile and support me in my decision, to hide how much he'll miss me. But he can't hide the fact that I just called him a burden, just as she has in veiled comments over the years. He's lost his ally, the one who understood. He's lost me.

While I was a student I visited home frequently but she always made sure she was out. Every time I called she handed the phone directly to him. Every time I asked him how she was, he said she was fine, clearly having been told that I was no longer privy to her life. My job took me further away, to other countries, and even when my visits home became sporadic, when we could only grow further apart, she made sure not to be there.

A village changes in fifteen years, grows, not quite in step with the cities, but it catches up. The main street has lost most of the shops from my childhood: greengrocer; florist; newsagent; bakery have all been replaced by one shiny new Co-op. Well, it's new to me, but I know Dad has probably told me about it in his letters. I love that my dad still writes letters and forgave his refusal to buy a computer and correspond via email.

"How can you feel what I'm saying on a computer screen, hen? You need to see my scrawl, to know it's really me, to smell the ink I use to scratch out our lives."

Always fancied himself as a writer, my dad, and who knows, maybe he should have given it a go. Maybe now it's too late.

I smell the salt and vinegar before I turn the corner in to our street. The chippy is still there, the window fogged up with the breath and impatience of the customers. It's Friday teatime so the queue stretches outside the door and a little way down the street, past the McPherson's front door. I know they still live there and wonder if Mrs McPherson still throws water over the drunks who nip out from the chippy for a quick pee in her doorway late on Saturday nights. I hope she does. And she'll know that I'm coming home. The whole street will know, just as they always knew everything. I imagine them peering out from behind their curtains, commenting on the suitcase I drag behind me, speculating on how much it holds, how long I plan to stay.

Mum and Dad have changed the front door since I was last here. It's the first thing everyone does when they buy their council house, thinking it makes it truly theirs, this tiny act of non-conformity. I use the glimmering gold coloured knocker – she hasn't let her standards slip – three short raps on the fake oak. She opens and my shock at seeing her as she is now is difficult to conceal. That's the trouble with hearing a voice on the phone; it doesn't prepare you for the way the person's body has aged. She's tiny. My big-boned, big-haired, ruddy-faced mum is tiny. The only thing I can do, the only thing that seems right, is hug her. I expect her to push me away but she doesn't. She doesn't go as far as to hug me back, but she leans into me for support. I feel her body quake as the tears start, but she controls them, controls herself, pulls away and tries to smile.

"There'll be time for that later. He's lost his speech and his right hand is weak, so he struggles to write, to tell me what he needs. Deep breath now, Eilidh. Deep breath, hen."

And I breathe – the smell of the mince she cooked for tea, the shampoo she used this morning and the hospital smell that never quite leaves even when the patient is home. I go into the living room where she has him settled as comfortably as she can and I know it'll be a long time before I leave home again.

Cowboys and Indians

He wakes up and goes into her room, hoping, just like yesterday and the day before, that it's a bad dream, that Grace'll be there, curled up, hidden under the duvet, waiting to jump out and hug him. The bed is flat, cold; covers unruffled.

He lies down, breathing in her scent from the pillow – strawberry shampoo – and cuddles her favourite bear. The Tiny Tears doll wearing the toy gun holster stares at him from the pink plastic chair in the corner of the room.

People tell him not to worry; at least she's with her mother. He can think of nothing worse.

#

It's strange being with Mum, but Grace gets used to it. An adventure, Mum promises. A chance to get to know each other again. Dad's happy about it, she says; needs a bit of time on his own. Grace thinks that's odd, but Mum wouldn't lie.

They finally stopped travelling last night. The old hotel smells fusty upstairs, especially in the corridors and near the toilets. The staff bedrooms are downstairs, along a passageway from the kitchen, so the rooms there smell of cooking. There are three of them including Mum: the Indian man – though not the kind with feathers and tepees, the other kind of Indian – and the man she thinks of as the cowboy because he wears boots with a raised heel and jeans and a checked shirt, just like the men in The High Chaparral and Bonanza. She's not sure if he wears the same colours because the television only shows things in black and white. She realises she'll miss her programmes and wonders if Dad is watching them alone.

There are no other women in the staff quarters. Most of the guests seem to be male, too; travelling salesmen, Mum says. The manager wasn't going to give Mum the chambermaid job until he saw Grace. He did that thing people always did when they looked at her – he went quiet, still, lost.

#

He never wanted to let her out of his sight. At first he thought it was just him, because she was his precious child, but he saw how other people looked at her swaying, shining hair, her smooth skin, her round, clear blue eyes, and that extra something he could never quite explain – a kind of light. He saw women captivated, grinning, desperate to touch her, to steal a piece of that light. But the men worried him – they couldn't look at her for long, had to look away, became agitated in her presence. He was sure they wanted more than her light. Over time he convinced himself he was wrong – one child could not turn all men to animals, not even a child like Grace.

Now he can't protect her and she's with someone who can't even look after herself.

#

Not going to school feels strange, but she gets used to it. Mum's lessons are fun – full of stories about kings and queens and gods. Mum's not too good with maths though and Grace worries she'll fall behind.

The manager asks about Grace and her schooling, but all Grace has to do is smile at him and he fidgets, then leaves them alone. She's always known she has this strange effect on people. Women adore her, always want to touch her hair, her cheek – anything they can – then they smile even more than they did before. Men stare at her, lose their voices, look like they're dreaming, then they can't look anymore.

The Indian tries to smile at her sometimes, but he gets shy and turns away. The cowboy is the only person she's ever met who seems to be unaffected by her. He doesn't smile – doesn't seem that interested in her – but he does look at Mum a lot. He smiles at Mum. They drink together at night, whisky, she thinks.

She likes the cowboy. It's nice to have someone to talk to, even if they don't really talk back. She asks him to teach her maths. He shrugs and grunts – would he be working in this kitchen if he was a maths teacher? She laughs. There's something about his voice, his grumpiness, that makes her laugh.

She asks Mum to get her some books of sums so she can keep up. Mum looks worried – we don't want to spend money on books, we want to save the money to get away from here.

Grace is confused. Away? Where to? For how long? When will we go home? She misses Dad, misses her friends. Mum hugs her – just enough for a holiday, then we'll go back, she promises.

#

He cooperates with the police, but it feels pointless. The house is so quiet when they leave. Friends visit, but they don't know what to say. His parents call from Aberdeen – should they come down to Glasgow? No, there's no point. Sarah's parents call to say how sorry they are. He thanks them, but he hates them, too. If they'd never had her...but then there would never have been Grace. Whatever else she did wrong, she gave him Grace. Now she's taken her back.

#

It's not as much fun as it was. Not being able to go out gets boring after a while. Mum looks more tense, older than just a few weeks ago when they left Glasgow. Grace has discovered that they're in Skegness. It's very cold and grey at this time of year.

The Indian talks to Mum a lot, always looking very sad. He tells her about India and Pakistan and something called partition. Grace doesn't understand, but Mum nods and pats his hand. He tells her about his wife and daughter, how he hasn't heard from them since he left his country. Mum cocks her head to one side and sighs with him.

This morning he gave Mum money and then they shook hands. Grace wonders what Mum has sold him and hopes it'll be enough money for their holiday so she can get back home. She wants to tell Dad about this adventure.

For the rest of the day the Indian avoids Grace – even more so than usual – while the cowboy follows Mum around and tries to get her to smile for him.

At bedtime Mum takes Grace's hands and looks serious. Don't worry, he won't hurt you, just do as he says and it'll be fine, I promise. Grace wants to ask what she means, but Mum shoves her to her room.

When Grace goes in, the Indian is there. Grace smiles at him. He smiles back, looks shy. He lies down on the bed and gestures for her to join him. She hesitates. He's a nice man, but this feels odd. Please, he says, lie here. She's so pleased and surprised that he actually speaks to her, she does as he says and edges onto the bed to lie down beside him. He puts his arm under her, pulls her so that she's lying with her back to him, him hugging her. He buries his head in her long hair, takes a deep breath then sighs. She feels him shake and knows he's crying. She tries to turn, to comfort him, but he stops her, holds her where she is, cries into her hair and calls her by a strange, beautiful name she's never heard before – just the name, over and over again.

When Grace wakes in the morning he's gone, as though he was never there. She goes to the kitchen and he's cooking breakfast, smiling. When he sees her he ruffles her hair, tells her to sit, to eat. He's talking to her, as if she's normal. It feels good. She smiles and hops up to the seat at the big table. The cowboy sees Grace and looks sad. He gives Mum an angry look. He says he has to fix a lock in one of the bedrooms and leaves.

Mum doesn't mention the Indian, the money, the holiday, or going home.

#

As days turn to weeks he becomes more desperate. He pesters the police, tells them they're slacking. He accuses relatives, friends, neighbours of colluding with Sarah, of helping her to steal Grace. They understand, they stand by him, but they stand just a little further away.

#

Since Grace's night with the Indian something has changed and the manager is able to talk to her a little. He's Irish and tells her stories of fairies and leprechauns. When he leaves he's always happy and sings strange songs in his lovely voice.

The Indian calls her by an Indian name now. She can't pronounce it and tells him, over and over, that her name is Grace, but he just laughs. It's their joke now, the thing they share.

Mum and the cowboy drink more and more whisky at night, but it doesn't seem to make them happy. They give each other dark looks and sometimes he grabs at Mum, but she shoves him away. Last night she called him 'jailbird' and he stomped out of the room.

#

He imagines Sarah drunk, unconscious, Grace wandering the lonely streets of an unknown town, prey for anyone who wants to take advantage. He can only sleep in her bed now, her old bear in his hands, its fur hard since so many of his tears have dried on its soft body. He can only see her face properly if he looks at photographs before he goes to bed. He's losing her.

#

When Grace sees the cowboy give Mum money, she knows he'll be in her room that night. But it's not the same as it was with the Indian – he shoves the money at Mum and they argue in spitting whispers until Mum nods and stuffs the money into her apron pocket.

At bedtime Mum doesn't tell her he'll be there or that it'll be all right, just pours herself a whisky. Grace goes to her room and there he is, waiting, but he doesn't look at her, which is strange since he's the only one who ever could. She smiles at him, touches his arm and asks if he's okay. He shoves her arm away and tells her to get on to the bed, but she doesn't 'cause this doesn't feel right. Are you going to stroke my hair and call me a funny but nice name then cry for a while? The cowboy's eyes shoot to hers and his mouth falls open. That's what he did? That's all he did in here with you? Grace nods. He drops his head and mutters Jesus over and over again and then he gets up and stumbles out of the room.

Grace climbs into bed, hoping she hasn't done anything wrong, hoping Mum won't be angry, but mostly hoping the cowboy will be okay. It takes her a long time to get to sleep.

Next morning the Indian is cooking and smiling, the manager is singing a happy song, Mum is upstairs cleaning a room and the cowboy has gone. What do they mean, 'gone'? Just gone, they say.

#

He waits, nervous, anxious. An anonymous tip, the police said. Some guy phoned, told them there was this child, he was worried – he described a child like Grace. The police are bringing her back. Back safe. Back home.

He sees her step out of the police car, rubbing her eyes – she always sleeps on a car journey – and he gulps back tears of relief. She looks at him, grins and runs towards him. He holds out his arms, but as she gets nearer his smile slips a little, his shoulders drop a fraction, his eyes narrow. She sees the change. Daddy? He forces the smile back onto his face and sweeps her up into his arms, sobbing onto her shoulder, telling her he loves her, he missed her, he's so glad she's home and everything will be all right now.

But there's something different, a tiny change that only he can see, and her light shines a little less brightly.